D1335176

SHACKLED TO THE PAST

Midwife Laura Morgan moves in next door to Dr Steve Drake with her daughter, Abby. Steve had lost his wife and daughter when both were drowned. He becomes very fond of Abby, and Laura begins to fall in love with him. But as the truth about the deaths of Steve's wife and child unfolds it seems that a happy future for them may never be possible, as long as he is haunted by the ghosts from the past.

Books by Teresa Ashby
in the Linford Romance Library:

TERESA ASHBY

SHACKLED
TO THE PAST

Complete and Unabridged

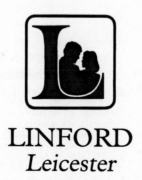

LINFORD
Leicester

First published in Great Britain in 2010

First Linford Edition
published 2012

British Library CIP Data

Ashby, Teresa.
    Shackled to the past.- -
    (Linford romance library)
    1. Love stories.
    2. Large type books.
    I. Title II. Series
    823.9'2–dc23

    ISBN 978–1–4448–1358–6

Published by
F. A. Thorpe (Publishing)
Anstey, Leicestershire

Set by Words & Graphics Ltd.
Anstey, Leicestershire
Printed and bound in Great Britain by
T. J. International Ltd., Padstow, Cornwall

This book is printed on acid-free paper

We do hope that you have enjoyed reading this large print book.

Did you know that all of our titles are available for purchase?

We publish a wide range of high quality large print books including:
Romances, Mysteries, Classics
General Fiction
Non Fiction and Westerns

Special interest titles available in large print are:
The Little Oxford Dictionary
Music Book, Song Book
Hymn Book, Service Book

Also available from us courtesy of Oxford University Press:
Young Readers' Dictionary
(large print edition)
Young Readers' Thesaurus
(large print edition)

For further information or a free brochure, please contact us at:
Ulverscroft Large Print Books Ltd.,
The Green, Bradgate Road, Anstey,
Leicester, LE7 7FU, England.
Tel: (00 44) 0116 236 4325
Fax: (00 44) 0116 234 0205

VERA'S VENTURE

Anne Holman

World War II is over, but new problems confront Vera. Her war-time job ends, and her husband Geoff is invalided out of the army and needs work. With two young children they must leave their home and move into a rundown cottage in Norfolk. Geoff has taken an engineering job with the Fen River Board. And whilst the river banks desperately need strengthening, floods are threatening the flat Fenlands, and Vera must protect her family.

1

Steve laughed as he watched Lucy running in circles around the sundial, her arms outstretched as she tried to catch a white butterfly that dipped and danced tantalisingly out of reach.

'You'll never catch it,' Tricia called out.

'I will,' Lucy cried and, as she redoubled her efforts, she lost her balance and staggered first this way then that, until she tripped over her own feet and tumbled, still giggling, to the ground. Tricia was there in an instant, hoisting the little girl up into her arms and holding her high in the air.

Lucy was a perfect little miniature of her mother. They both had bright green eyes and soft red hair, though Tricia's was slightly darker. Steve laughed, his heart full to bursting.

'You're back,' he said. 'This time I won't mess up.'

He emerged from sleep with a warm smile on his face. He hadn't smiled like that since ... They're dead, they're both dead, he told himself harshly as his eyes finally opened. You can't see them. They aren't here. You will never see them again. He struggled against waking, knowing that only in his dreams would he ever see his wife and child again. The cold chill in the air wrapped round him like a shroud and he shivered.

But the laughter continued. It was just feet away from the garden hammock where he'd sat to gather his thoughts, and in the peace and quiet of his garden had dozed off. He sat upright and shook his head. Now he was fully awake he could hear more noises. Doors banging, men shouting and still the child's laughter. He staggered to his feet and walked down the side of the cottage to the front.

There was a large removal van

parked in the lane and men in white overalls hurrying in and out of the empty cottage next door. So someone was moving in at last.

He tried to shake off the dream, but the child's laughter rang out again, right behind him now, and he spun round, rushing back into his garden. He ran past the hammock and through the shrubs that divided his large garden in two only to stop dead in his tracks.

She was right in the middle of the lower lawn running rings around the sundial and the sight of her knocked the breath out of him. For a split second he thought . . .

She turned to face him and stopped giggling abruptly, her huge eyes positively brimming with mischief. Her hair had looked red in the autumn sun, but as a cloud passed across the sun the colour faded from copper to yellow gold. The child was small and skinny with long curls cascading down her back. She wore jeans and a bright pink jacket.

Then he saw what she'd been chasing. A large silver tabby cat with vivid green eyes. It shrank to the ground at the sight of him, then turned and bolted down the garden with the child in pursuit.

'Wait,' he called. 'Stop! Don't go down there.'

*   *   *

Laura had left Abby in her new bedroom unpacking her toys while she supervised the removers. 'Tea's ready,' she called and the four men trooped into her kitchen, rubbing their hands together.

'Where do you want this, love?' one of them asked, dangling a cat basket in the air.

'Just here will be fine,' Laura said, frowning. 'I swear I put the box in the sitting room. I don't want Sam to get out just yet in case he runs off.'

The men exchanged looks. 'Too late for that,' the one holding the basket said flicking the door open. 'It's empty.'

'Oh, no. How did that happen?'

'At a guess I'd say your little girl let him out,' he replied with good humour. 'The last time I saw her, she was carrying the basket outside.'

Laura turned and rushed upstairs but, as she feared, Abby's room was empty. She raced to the window and flung it open looking out over the back garden, but there was no sign of her daughter or the cat. She was gripped with panic, all too aware of the close proximity of the river to their back garden. Water always drew children. What if Abby had wandered down there and . . . no, it didn't bear thinking about.

With a cry of desperation, Laura ran downstairs and out of the front door. She looked up and down the lane, then she ran back through the house into the garden and at once saw the hole in the fence.

★   ★   ★

5

Steve closed his eyes for a second and swayed unsteadily. His mouth was so dry he couldn't speak and his limbs felt like lead. This is ridiculous, he told himself. She didn't even look like Lucy. But what on earth was she doing in his garden — and why in heaven's name did she have to head that way? He'd just started after her when he heard a voice.

'Abby . . . Abby!'

He looked over the fence and saw a young, slightly-built woman with almost black hair falling in unruly tendrils over her shoulders.

'This way,' he called, pointing at the hole in the fence that the child must have used to gain access.

'Where is she? I'm so sorry,' she said as she clambered through the hole. 'I told her not to leave the garden.'

'You can't tell a child of that age anything and expect them to understand,' he said sharply. 'But we have to find her — fast.'

She looked startled. 'I know, but . . . '

'But nothing. Have you any idea how dangerous this place is?'

'Yes I have, actually,' she said. 'Which is why I must find her. But I don't see what you have to be so angry about.'

He blinked hard. He was tired but — hell's teeth — children were precious, you couldn't let them out of your sight not even for an instant, didn't she realise that?

'It's a tidal river,' he said. 'There are deadly currents. Grown men have drowned. What chance do you think a little girl . . . ' He couldn't continue. The pain was too much, even now, after five long years. He wouldn't have thought it possible, but seeing that little girl had brought it all back as if it had only happened yesterday.

'I'm not stupid,' she snapped. 'Which way did she go?'

'I have no idea,' he said. 'You take the right path towards the wood, I'll head down to the river. And hurry!'

He ran down towards the river and could have wept with relief when he

7

saw Abby sitting on the bank stroking the cat which was sitting in her lap.

'All right, honey?' he said softly. The last thing he wanted to do was startle her. 'You shouldn't be down here on your own.'

'Is this place yours?'

'No, anyone can come here, but you really mustn't come to the river without an adult. It can be very dangerous. Will you come with me now and I'll take you home? Your Mummy is very worried about you.'

She gave him a wary look then smiled.

'Okay,' she said scrambling to her feet. 'Mummy says I mustn't talk to strangers, but you're not really a stranger because you live next door. I saw you sleeping in the garden. My name's Abby.'

'I'm Steve,' he said almost choking on the emotion rising in his throat.

She held the cat up to him and he took him from her and carried him in the crook of one arm, holding Abby's tiny hand with his free hand.

There was the crackle of dry twigs and the sound of someone out of breath, then Abby's mother came tearing round the comer. 'There was no sign of her — Oh! Thank goodness, you've got her. I was so frightened. Abby why on earth did you run off like that?' She scooped Abby up into her arms. 'I'm really sorry about this, Mr . . . '

'Steve,' he said. 'You really should be more careful.'

She gave him an exasperated look. 'Thank you for finding her,' she said coolly. 'I can assure you this won't happen again. Abby and I will be having a long talk. Please excuse us.'

She put Abby down, then took the cat from him and hurried on up the shady path ahead of him with Abby running along beside her. Just before they disappeared round the corner, Abby turned and gave him a little smile and a wave. He smiled and waved back.

Just a small gesture, but it damn near tore the heart right out of him.

Laura had to fight the tears as she hurried Abby back to the house. What a great start to their new life this was — and what an inauspicious way to meet her new neighbour.

'Steve's nice isn't he?' Abby said.

'Nice?' Not the word she would have chosen. Good looking in a rugged, almost dangerous sort of way, but she would have someone a bit more friendly as her next door neighbour if she could have chosen. She just hoped his wife was a bit friendlier.

Some time later, Laura sat on the floor amid a pile of boxes and packing cases and heaved a sigh. Abby had crashed out ages ago on her bed upstairs, curled up with Sam who had made himself completely at home.

She wiped her hand across her face, leaving a dirty smudge on her cheek then got up and went to the window. She hadn't realised quite how close the river was or that it was so easily accessible from the gardens. The water looked silvery grey and very still and wide through the bare branches of the trees. She'd have to speak to Abby about it, make sure she understood the dangers, but there would always be a risk that Abby would forget.

She'd viewed the cottage at the end of the summer. Back then she'd seen the river from the lane leading to the cottage. It had been a beautiful deep shade of blue. Living in the woods near a river down by an old disused railway line and with just one other neighbour had seemed very appealing back then. But that was before she met the neighbour.

'I'm not going to worry about the river,' Laura said out loud.

While Laura was at work, Abby would be with her Aunt Claire, Laura's older sister. It had been Claire's idea that Laura should move here and be closer to family.

'They're advertising for a midwife at Banford Lodge,' Claire had told her excitedly. 'It's near us. I could easily look after Abby for you.'

Claire had never really approved of Laura continuing to work after Abby was born, but when Tim walked out on them, he'd left Laura no choice. So here she was. The job was hers and she'd found herself somewhere to live. She had a week to knock the place into some kind of order and, with her brother-in-law Mike's help, she'd soon have it shipshape.

But right now there was something she had to do. She went out to the shed and found some half decent looking bits of wood and carried them across to the hole in the fence.

She'd make sure Abby didn't wander into Steve's garden again.

* * *

Next door, Steve put aside the newspaper he'd been reading and sighed wearily. A door closing next door gave him a start. He'd become used to

12

having this place to himself, but had always known his happy solitude would come to an end one day.

He didn't even know the adjoining cottage had been sold since the For Sale sign had long since been swallowed up in that jungle of a garden and, as far as he knew, no one had been to view. He had once considered buying it himself and knocking the two houses into one, turning it into a real family home, but that was before, when he had a family, and now there was simply no point.

Out in the kitchen, he switched on the kettle and drummed his fingers on the worktop as he waited for it to boil. It was traditional, wasn't it, to make hot drinks for the new neighbours? It was a neighbourly gesture and he felt it might go some way to making amends for them getting off on the wrong foot earlier. He supposed he had come across as a bit bad tempered.

A bit . . . He smiled wryly. The poor

woman must be wondering what on earth she'd let herself in for. As he set out mugs on a tray, he spotted something moving in the back garden and when he looked up, his breath caught in his throat. Now what was the crazy woman up to?

When he'd finished making the tea, he walked down to the fence where she was beavering away with hammer and nails and a few scraps of wood. As he approached, she regarded him warily.

'What are you doing?' he asked her.

'What does it look like?' she said. 'If I fix this fence, then Abby won't trouble you again. It's easier to do it from this side.'

'You don't get it do you? I don't mind her coming into the garden, in fact she's more than welcome until you can sort your own garden out. I just wanted to make sure you understood how dangerous the river is.'

'I'm not stupid,' she murmured. She lowered her eyes, the dark sweep of her lashes brushing against the flushed curve of her cheek. He felt sorry for her. Moving house was a stressful enough business without finding yourself living next door to Mr Grumpy.

'People come here, they think it's wonderful being so close to the river and they just don't realise . . . '

'I said, I'm not stupid,' she said, eyes flashing.

This wasn't going well. He hadn't intended to start arguing with her. 'I've just made a pot of tea if you'd like some,' he said.

She hesitated for a moment, then frowned as if trying to make sense of him. 'I'd love one,' she said at last and then she smiled and it was as if all the air had been sucked out of him. Phew, that was unexpected. Maybe he was more tired than he'd realised. 'I'll just finish this,' she said.

'Leave it. I'll sort it out for you later.'

'I'm perfectly capable,' she said, the smile disappearing.

'I'm sure you are,' he said. 'But that

wood you're using is rotten.'

'Oh,' she said. 'I hadn't realised.'

'The tea is getting cold,' he said. 'I'm sorry, I didn't catch your name.'

'Laura,' she said. 'Abby's just having a nap. She'll be waking soon, so is it okay if I bring her round for that tea?'

'Sure,' he said. 'Will your husband be coming with you?'

'I don't have a husband,' she murmured, looking away.

2

There had definitely been a woman's touch in the cottage at some time, but Laura guessed it was probably several years ago. The fabrics were all very pretty, but rather faded and out of date. And the cottage itself was clean and tidy, but as a home it lacked warmth. A bit like its owner.

Abby was polite and charming and on her best behaviour. They sat on stools and watched as Steve poured two mugs of tea and a glass of milk for Abby. Hopefully this would be Laura's chance to convince him she wasn't the idiot he thought she was.

'Excuse me,' he said when his mobile phone rang and he answered it. 'Yes. I'll be right there.' He hung up.

'That must be the quickest phone call ever,' Laura said.

'I'm so sorry, but I have to go out,' he

replied, his mind clearly on other things. 'Please finish your tea and just drop the latch on your way out.' And with that, he was gone.

* * *

Steve couldn't believe his eyes when he got back home and found his kitchen neat and tidy and the washing-up done.

Sleep, that's what he needed, and plenty of it. He stumbled up the stairs and sprawled out on his bed fully clothed, staring up at the ceiling. But tired as he was, he couldn't sleep. Every time he closed his eyes, all he could see was Laura and Abby and if he tried to put them out of his mind, Tricia and Lucy appeared instead.

He was going to have to tread very carefully and keep his distance. In the house next door lay heartbreak and pain. It had already started. He wasn't going to let it get any worse.

Over the next few days, Steve tried to ignore the comings and goings next door, but again and again he found himself at the window.

Who was the man who spent so much time there . . . the child's father or just the mother's lover — and why should he care anyway? He was a busy man, too busy to waste time speculating about the lives of strangers. By the end of that first week, he knew nothing more about Laura and Abby than he'd known at the beginning and that was the way he wanted it to stay.

When he opened his front door and saw Laura in the arms of the burly man right out on the front path he stepped straight back inside and closed the door quietly.

He was walking away from the door, back towards the kitchen, when he heard the letter box slap open. Spinning round, he saw a pair of bright blue eyes peering in at him.

'Have you seen Sam?'

He went back to the door and crouched down, peeking back through the letterbox. 'Sam?'

'My cat. He's the tabby, remember? Uncle Mike said he saw him coming into your garden again.'

'I haven't seen him,' he said. 'But I'll look out for him. He's probably hiding away somewhere and will come home when he's hungry.'

'That's what Mummy says.'

'Abby!' He heard Laura's voice call out, then the letterbox clattered shut in his face and he heard Abby's frantic footsteps beating a retreat down the path. By the time he was on his feet with the door open, Abby was in her mother's arms.

'What were you doing, bothering Steve? I told you not to wander off on your own,' Laura scolded her daughter.

'I was looking for Sam,' Abby cried. 'Uncle Mike said he saw him going next door.'

'I haven't seen your cat, Abby,' Steve called over. 'But if I do, I'll bring him home to you, don't worry.' He strolled towards her, his hands thrust deep in his pockets as Abby bounded back into the cottage. The guy Abby had called Uncle Mike had driven off.

'She just slipped out of my sight for a moment,' Laura said defensively.

'That's all it takes, you know,' he said. 'Just a moment. Perhaps you should spend a little less time on loving goodbyes with your boyfriend and more watching your child.'

'What?' she gasped.

He turned and walked back inside, his heart pounding. If there was a line he'd just pole vaulted right over it. What on earth possessed him to say such a thing? He was behaving like an interfering old busy-body with nothing better to do than spy on his neighbour. From now on, he vowed, he'd keep his nose out of Laura's business.

★ ★ ★

Laura started her new job at the maternity unit a week after moving in to the cottage. Her first shift was the night shift. Thank goodness for Claire and her spare bed, she thought. At least she knew that Abby was safe.

She had walked in with a mixture of excitement and nervousness, but Susan, the on-duty healthcare assistant, put her immediately at her ease.

The night was quiet until about midnight when the phone rang.

'Maternity, Sister Morgan speaking,' Laura said.

'I'm bringing my wife in,' an anxious voice declared with urgency. 'She's having a baby.'

'All right,' Laura smiled. 'Could you tell me her name?' She reached for a pen and jotted down some details. 'Bring her in without delay Mr Fisher.'

A short while later, the bell rang; she hurried down the corridor to answer the door and was confronted with a terrified looking man apparently supporting his wife. As they stumbled through the door, it was all too obvious that it was the other way around.

'Hi, I'm Alyson Fisher. My husband called a few minutes ago to say we were on our way in. He's been so worried,' she explained. 'I don't think he's slept for the past week. Poor love, it's all been too much for him.'

'He'll be all right, Alyson,' Laura's immediate concern was for mother and baby. 'Sit down there, Mr Fisher. I'll come and fetch you in a minute.'

'Thank you,' he said weakly and it was only as their eyes met, that Laura and Alyson both burst out laughing.

'You wouldn't believe he plays rugby. He's been even worse since I've been so close to my due date. I've practically had to push him out of the house to go to work every — ' She stopped and gasped, her eyes widening and Laura waited for the contraction to pass.

'Let's have you up on the bed. Shall I give you a hand? There, comfy?' Alyson nodded and Laura began her examination. Labour had started, but it would be a while before the baby was born. 'I'll put you in a side ward and your husband can sit with you until things are a little further along,' Laura said reassuringly.

John Fisher had abandoned his chair and was pacing the corridor.

'Mr Fisher, would you like to come this way?' Laura suggested.

'Why is she in here on her own — is something wrong?' he demanded when Laura took him to the side ward.

'We'll move Alyson when she's a little further on,' Laura explained patiently. 'For the moment, she'll be more comfortable in here.'

'But she's about to have a baby.'

'John, please . . . ' Alyson whispered. 'Don't make such a fuss. Sister Morgan knows what she's doing.'

'You're new aren't you?' he said. 'How long have you been a midwife?'

'Please try not to worry, Mr Fisher,' Laura said. 'Your wife is fine and everything is as it should be.'

'Hold on,' John Fisher chased her out of the room. 'Nurse, you can't leave her like that. Aren't you going to do something?'

'Mr Fisher,' Laura swung round to face him. He towered over her, a huge man, red in the face, very frightened. 'Please try to stay calm. It may not seem so to you, but everything is progressing as it should.' Laura smiled warmly. He did have his wife's best interests at heart, it wouldn't be fair to hold that against him. 'Please, Mr Fisher, the best you can do for your wife right now, is just be there for her. I'll take good care of her when the time comes, I promise.'

'How's our new arrival?' Susan asked when Laura returned.

'Very straightforward. I see she's one of Dr Drake's patients.'

'Yes, lucky girl.' Susan remarked. 'Have you met him yet?'

'Not yet,' Laura said.

'He's gorgeous,' Susan said. 'Tall, dark, handsome . . . '

'Susan! And you with two grown up children and two grandchildren.' Laura laughed. 'Shame on you!'

'He's got the most incredible blue

eyes,' Susan went on, unabashed.

'Oh, I see,' Laura said. 'A real heartthrob. I'm going to have to keep an eye on you with him around if he's as gorgeous as you say.'

'He is,' Susan sighed. 'Unfortunately he isn't available. Well I mean he's single, but he's off women, apparently.'

'A woman hater?'

'Oh, no,' Susan laughed. 'Definitely not that. He's lovely — oh, you'll know what I mean once you meet him.'

'Who can that be?' Laura jumped when the bell rang to signal someone arriving in the unit. She hurried down the long corridor towards the entrance. As she passed the side ward where Alyson Fisher was dozing, she saw John Fisher coming out behind her.

The inner door was flung open and a man marched in. Laura looked beyond him expectantly, but quickly realised he was alone. A little tremor of fear started in her gut. What did this wild-looking stranger want and how did he gain access to the unit? She turned to confront him, but he had his back to her, talking with John Fisher.

'Excuse me,' she said indignantly. 'I'm sorry, but you can't just walk in here in the middle of the night and — ' He turned to look at her with icy blue eyes. Laura's knees went weak. 'You!' She gasped.

His cold look turned blank for a moment as he continued staring at her. The lights in the corridor suddenly seemed too bright and Laura had to close her eyes. I must be dreaming, she thought desperately, or having a nightmare. Surely this can't be real, this can't be him.

At last, the light of recognition dawned in his eyes and he frowned as he said, 'Laura?'

★ ★ ★

There was no mistaking those big, smoky-grey eyes or that cute upturned nose — it was his new neighbour. He hadn't realised at first; she looked so

27

different in uniform and with her unruly hair all neatly pinned back. So this was why she was out every night — not that he was interested of course . . . who was he trying to kid?

'I don't believe it,' she whispered, aghast. 'What are you doing here?'

'Sister Morgan I presume,' he said. 'I'm Steve Drake. I understand that you have one of my patients here in advanced labour. Is she in here?' he headed towards the delivery suite.

'No, she is not in there,' Laura finally found her voice and was grateful that it sounded firm and steady. 'Mrs Fisher is in the side ward.'

'You see,' John Fisher cried triumphantly. 'I told you, Doctor, I told you that she was ignoring us.'

'You called Dr Drake out?' Laura said, shocked.

'I did, indeed,' John Fisher snorted. 'I had to do something.'

Annoyed as she was, Laura couldn't help warming to Mr Fisher. At least he cared enough to try to do something.

Tim hadn't even been present at Abby's birth. He couldn't have shown less interest in it all if he'd been a complete stranger.

'Mr Fisher, I can assure you that your wife will receive the attention she needs when she needs it. As for you, Dr Drake, I would have called you if and when your attendance was required.'

Alyson's buzzer went and Laura hurried into the side ward followed closely by Steve.

'Getting stronger,' Alyson said. 'Closer together. Hi, Dr Drake.'

'Hi Alyson,' he smiled warmly and checked the monitors. 'It's all looking good here.'

'I'm glad to hear it. Are you convinced now that I can do my job?'

'There was never any doubt that you — ' he began.

'Weren't there? You really do have a low opinion of me don't you?'

'But I didn't know you were Sister Morgan,' he protested. 'You've got it all wrong, Laura. This is the last place on earth I expected to find you.' She stared at him until the shadow of a smile crossed his face. 'I'm sorry,' his smile died on his lips as she continued to glare at him. 'I didn't know what else to think when Fisher called me. He sounded in such a panic.'

He took a step towards her, his tone and expression conciliatory. 'Laura, we haven't worked together before. It's bound to take time to — '

'Excuse me,' Laura said stiffly. 'I have work to do. It won't be long now, Alyson. Perhaps you'd like to stay, Doctor.'

His face broke into a grin. 'I'd love to,' he said.

'What's going on, what's happening?' John Fisher came into the room and demanded, his face pinched with worry.

'It's all right, Mr Fisher,' Steve assured the distraught man as he ushered him outside. 'Sister Morgan has everything under control. We're going to move Alyson to the delivery suite in a little while, so why don't you come with me and we'll gown up.'

It was hard to believe that this capable woman was the same one that rattled around in the cottage next door in baggy, paint-splattered cargo pants and who had attempted to fix fences with worm-riddled old wood. The one woman in the world he would have said was totally disorganised and yet, watching her at work here, she was completely in control. His lips curved in a smile just as she looked up and he saw a blaze of colour rush to her cheeks before she turned quickly away.

Half an hour later, things had progressed rapidly and Alyson's contractions were coming one on top of another until at last her baby girl was born. 'Now she's finally here. I can hardly believe it,' Alyson cried. 'Look, John, see how beautiful she is . . . '

The rest was routine. John Fisher sat on a chair, a vacant look on his face as he gazed down at the baby in his arms. He looked shell-shocked and every so often, his eyes would brim with tears and he'd sniff loudly.

'She's beautiful,' Laura said

'Thank you,' he looked up at her and whispered. 'I'm sorry about, well, you know. I . . . I've never had a baby before.'

'You're welcome,' Laura smiled.

★ ★ ★

'Have you time for a coffee before you go, Dr Drake?' Susan asked as he followed Laura into her office once the Fishers were settled on the ward.

'I'd love one.'

'One for you, Laura?' Susan asked.

'Please,' Laura said and sat down at her desk.

'I'm sorry about earlier,' Steve said.

'Forget it,' Laura replied, without looking up.

'I would, but I don't think you have.'

'It's forgotten, believe me.' She felt him staring at her and looked up. 'Okay, yes, I did feel annoyed that you should assume I wasn't doing my job properly,' she admitted. 'But looking at it from your point of view, you received a call from a panic-stricken father in the middle of the night and couldn't very well ignore it. You're forgiven, Dr Drake.'

'Thanks,' he said. 'I'd just like to ask one more thing.'

'Go ahead.'

'Please, call me Steve.'

'I don't think . . . '

'Do you really dislike me that much?' he asked despondently.

'I don't dislike you. What on earth makes you think that?' Dislike him? If only she did. If anything she was bewildered that he seemed to dislike her and had done so from the minute he set eyes on her. 'It's just that you're the last person I expected to come walking in through that door. I had no idea that you were Dr Drake. If I had . . . '

'What?' he teased, his blue eyes twinkling. 'What would you have done if you had known who I was, Laura?'

She didn't know. Run a mile maybe. 'Do you like working here?' he went on, not waiting for an answer.

'So far,' she nodded. 'It's very different to my last hospital. I rarely got to see a pregnancy through from beginning to end as we had such a huge unit, but hopefully that won't happen here.'

'Think you'll stay?'

'I don't see why not.'

'Good — so no plans for giving up to add to your family?'

She looked up at the ceiling and laughed. 'If that's your way of finding out if I'm in a relationship . . . '

'Why should I want to do that?' he asked, making her feel silly for making such an assumption. 'Although I admit I'm curious — what happened to Abby's father? Or was that him you were in a passionate clinch with outside your cottage the other day?'

The attitude was back. The one that said he didn't like her very much.

'Abby's father and I split up when

she was four weeks old,' she replied, her voice trembling. She didn't mean it to, after all she was over all that now wasn't she? 'Does that satisfy your curiosity?'

'I wasn't asking out of idle curiosity,' he said at last, his voice gruff. 'I was simply trying to make conversation. I apologise. I was out of order. I'm not very good at this kind of small talk. I'm out of practice.'

'No problem,' she said at last, straightening some papers on her desk.

'Good,' he smiled and Laura felt an odd jolt deep down inside. That smile of his had a disquieting knack of making her heart beat faster.

3

When Laura got home, she switched on the electric heater and pulled it closer to the armchair where she sat and kicked off her shoes. There was no point taking off her coat until the cottage had warmed up.

She must have dozed, for the slamming of a car door woke her with a start and she found she was uncomfortably hot now. Head fuzzy, she got to her feet and shed her coat and found herself listening as Steve let himself in to the cottage next door. The walls were thin and she heard his every movement. Normally she didn't notice, for when Abby was here, the cottage was never this quiet. He went into the kitchen and she heard the clatter of crockery as he prepared breakfast.

'Well, surely you've better things to do than listen to him all day,' she rebuked herself and, shaking her head, she climbed the stairs to the bathroom to run herself a hot bath.

Closing her eyes, she let the hot soapy water soothe her aching limbs. And then she heard noises next door, from his bathroom adjoined hers, but she guessed from the sounds that he was taking a shower rather than having a soak. And he was singing.

He had a beautiful voice too, so clear and tuneful that if she closed her eyes, it was as if he was in the room with her. It was mesmerising and when the rush of water stopped, so did the singing. She stood up, grabbed a towel and clapped furiously. There was a brief silence, then she heard his low, throaty chuckle and imagined him bowing to the wall.

A little later, before going to bed for the day, she popped into the garden in her dressing gown to search for the cat. 'Sam,' she called, rattling a box of dried cat food.

Almost at once, a tousled head

popped up on the other side of the fence. 'He's over here,' Steve said with a grin. 'I'm afraid he's caught something and taken it deep into the hedge.'

'Oh, no,' Laura groaned. 'He's such a monster. There's no need for him to catch anything — he gets more than enough to eat. Was it dead?'

'Definitely.'

'Thank goodness,' she sighed.

'It's in their nature,' he said with a philosophical air. 'You won't change that. Aren't you cold?'

She realised then that she was in her dressing gown and pulled it more closely around herself. 'A bit,' she admitted. 'I'm about to go to bed and I wanted the cat to come in for his breakfast. He'll probably wait until I've just dropped off then wake me up, demanding I feed him.'

Steve's eyes swept around the garden and she realised he was looking for something. 'Where's Abby?' he asked.

It was a simple enough question, but it made Laura prickle with resentment.

Twice now he'd been off with her about not watching Abby properly — was he about to do it again?

Fighting to keep her voice level, she replied, 'Abby is with my sister. Why? Did you think I'd mislaid her and not realised?'

'Of course not,' he said, but the two red spots that appeared in his cheeks told a different story. That's exactly what he had thought. He'd made up his mind that she was a complete failure as a mother and it seemed that nothing she did or said would change his opinion.

But wasn't that exactly what she was? A complete failure — at least as far as her private life was concerned. To her dismay tears started to gather in her eyes. She thought she was over all that, but somehow Steve Drake had stirred up all sorts of feelings inside her.

'So if Abby's not here,' he said with a grin, 'then it must have been you clapping in the bathroom.' She flushed. 'Glad you enjoyed it. Here, give me the cat food,' he said, reaching across the fence. 'I'll feed him for you when he's hungry and I'll give him a saucer of milk. You'd better get some rest. You look all in.'

She passed him the box and as he took it, his hand brushed against hers and she withdrew her hand quickly as if it had been scalded.

'You don't have to be so scared of me, Laura,' he murmured.

'What makes you think I'm scared?' She laughed lightly, but it came out sounding false and she wished with all her heart she hadn't bothered.

'Body language, love,' he replied. 'You're frightened to death and there's really no need. I've no interest in you apart from a neighbourly one.' How embarrassing. Did he really think she was attracted to him? The conceited . . . 'Oops,' he grimaced. 'I didn't mean it to sound like that. What I meant to say was I'm . . . '

'Steve, I don't really care,' she said wearily. 'I'm tired and I'm going to go to bed now.'

Nights were too quiet for Laura's liking. She worked at her best when pushed to her limits, which she was during the day. She was relieved when her shift changed back to days.

'I hear you had a run in with Doctor Drake,' Caroline Henderson declared when Laura walked into the unit.

'A misunderstanding,' Laura said warily.

'That's not like him,' Caroline said, frowning. 'He's usually lovely.'

'So everyone keeps telling me,' Laura said.

'Look, Laura I don't want to speak out of turn, but don't get any ideas about Steve. He's a good looking guy and no one would blame you for — '

'Hold on,' Laura was dismayed. 'You've got this wrong.'

'Good,' Caroline smiled. 'Just warning you that's all. You wouldn't be the first to fall for him.'

'The last thing I want to do is get

romantically involved with anyone.'

Their conversation was interrupted when one of the healthcare assistants rushed in to say someone on the ward was sick.

'Oh no,' Caroline groaned. 'The norovirus. I thought we'd escaped.'

'I'll inform the General,' Laura said. 'We won't be able to take in any new admissions. We'll have to shut the unit down.'

* * *

Over the following few days, Laura saw very little of Steve Drake — except when she looked into the garden and saw him chatting to Abby over the fence. Today, Abby was playing outside on her own, wrapped up against the cold and just pottering around as small children do.

Smiling, Laura turned from the window and drew some freshly baked scones from the oven. When she'd finished setting them out on a cooling

42

rack, she turned back to the window to call Abby in. By the time she'd got out of her outdoor clothes and washed her hands, the scones would be cool enough to eat.

But there was no sign of Abby in the garden and Laura felt a sudden stab of alarm. She dropped the oven glove she was holding onto the floor and raced outside, almost wilting with relief when she heard Abby's happy giggles drifting through from next door.

Looking over the fence, she could see Abby in Steve's garden, standing at the foot of an oak tree looking up. Steve was high up in the branches reaching out towards Sam, who was perched there, a nonchalant and rather snooty look on his face.

He hadn't done anything about the fence as yet and Laura clambered through the hole and joined Abby at the foot of the tree. She had to suppress a giggle. Surely he hadn't fallen for that one. Cats rarely got stuck up trees, least of all agile climbers like Sam.

'What are you doing up there?' Laura asked calmly.

The sound of her voice made him jump and he almost lost his footing. The branches swayed and he wobbled, but finally he regained his balance and glanced down at her. 'I'm trying to rescue your cat.'

'What makes you think he needs rescuing?' Laura teased, a twinkle in her eye. 'He's probably better at climbing trees than you are.'

'Thanks for the vote of confidence.' He chuckled. 'I'm risking life and limb up here I'll have you know.'

'I asked Steve to rescue Sam,' Abby said.

'Did you try calling him?' Laura asked with a grin and received her reply in Abby's sheepish smile. 'I thought not. Sam . . . Sam, come on.'

Sam perked up and shot down the trunk of the tree, landing at the bottom and winding himself around Laura's legs, purring furiously.

Steve followed, coming down more slowly and finally jumping the last few feet to end up standing right in front of her. She was afraid he'd be cross, but to her immense relief, he was grinning. She reached out automatically and tugged a twig from his hair.

'You know I feel a complete idiot now?' he said ruefully.

'There's no need,' she smiled. 'Abby told you the cat was stuck — what else were you to do? Oh, you've cut your hand.'

'It's nothing,' he said, curling his fingers into a fist and hiding the bloody wound in his palm. 'Just a scratch.'

'Let me see,' Laura insisted and prised his fingers open with an exasperated sigh. 'Stop fighting me. Honestly, you're worse than a child.' Gently she examined the cut and pronounced, 'It's just a scratch.'

'That's just what I — ' he began, saw she was laughing and joined in.

'We should clean it though,' she added more seriously. 'Come on through to our place. I think climbing trees to rescue errant felines deserves a little first aid don't you?'

They went back through the hole in the fence and it was Abby who said, 'We should put a proper gate in.'

Her remark made Steve laugh and Laura blush. It hinted at more such comings and goings and Laura wasn't sure that's what she wanted, particularly after her earlier conversation with Caroline.

In her warm, cosy kitchen he sat perched on a stool at the breakfast bar while she cleaned the cut on his hand. It meant she had to hold his hand in hers and she found herself noticing his long, slender fingers.

'Kiss it better.' Abby demanded. 'Like you do with me when I've got a hurt. Go on, Mummy.'

Steve's face broke into a craggy grin.

'It doesn't need to be kissed,' Laura said shortly, pressing down the lid on the first aid box.

'Please, Mummy,' Abby begged. 'It always helps me to feel better.'

Her eyes met Steve's. He smiled and shrugged. 'Worth a try,' he said. 'It does sting quite a bit.'

'You're ganging up on me.' Laura said, but she found herself entering into the spirit of the thing and she raised his hand to her lips. And then it happened. Her eyes met his and this time she was frozen there, his hand still against her lips. She couldn't breathe. She dropped his hand. Whatever this thing was that she was feeling she didn't want to be feeling it, least of all for him when it certainly wasn't likely to be reciprocated.

'I drew a picture for you,' Abby said, grabbing Steve's good hand and dragging him towards the sitting room. 'Come and see it.'

Seconds later, there was the soft rumble of his laughter. It gave Laura time to assemble her disordered thoughts — not much time, but enough for the colour to die in her cheeks and for her heart to stop racing wildly. By the time she went through to the sitting room, Steve was galloping round the floor on his hands and knees with Abby riding on his back, whooping and squealing while he whinnied like a horse.

Abby's laughter warmed her heart and she found herself joining in, then suddenly it was as if he'd only just become aware of her presence and he stopped and gently eased Abby off his back and stood up. He looked almost ashamed of himself.

Laura frowned. 'What's wrong?'

'Nothing,' he muttered, pressing his fingers into his forehead. 'Everything . . . excuse me, Laura, I've got to run. I shouldn't even be here.'

He pressed his hands on her shoulders for a moment, gave her a regretful smile then hurried off.

Laura tried to shrug off his sudden departure and the way it had hurt her and tried to explain it to Abby. 'He's a very busy doctor,' she said. 'He probably remembered he was meant to be somewhere else.'

But no matter how many times she looked out of the window that day, his car remained parked outside. Steve Drake was going nowhere.

★   ★   ★

At last, the unit was clear of the virus and completely empty of patients. All cases had been diverted to the general hospital. Laura had never seen it so quiet. But not for long. At any moment, five mothers complete with babies were due to arrive from the general, to spend the rest of their confinement in the unit.

She went into one of the two wards and shook out the curtains, straightening the folds so they hung neatly. Stopping, she looked out of the window across the lawns. How grand this place must have been a hundred years or so ago when it belonged to just one family.

A grey mist was rolling across the grass, skimming the surface. Above and beyond it, where the mist was thinner, she could see the pale yellow orb of the sun. Once the mist cleared, it would be a beautiful autumn day, bright and clear. She heaved a sigh and thought how beautiful the world could be, even in the middle of a cold and bleak autumn.

'That was a deep sigh.'

She spun round and came face to face with Steve. 'How long have you been standing there?'

'When I arrived, you were fiddling with the curtain, getting it to hang just so. For someone who doesn't know a lump of rotten wood when it's right under her nose, you can be incredibly precise.'

'You're never going to let me forget that, are you?'

He threw back his head and laughed. He had a deep, resonant laugh and it left her feeling puzzled and vulnerable. Why was he laughing at her? Was she really so funny? He stopped laughing and regarded her seriously for a moment. Then he reached out and clamped both hands on her upper arms. Their eyes met. Did he know how much she was attracted to him? She hadn't felt this way for years and had never expected to. And now, of all people, it had to be him that awoke feelings she had long since thought dead and buried.

'You think I'm some kind of joke,' she said.

He held her for a moment more, then dropped his hands. 'Is that what you think?' Tiny lines appeared along his forehead as he frowned. 'That I'm laughing at you? Nothing could be further from the truth.'

'Then what, Steve? I don't even know whether you like me or not.'

'Like you?' he rasped.

Of course he didn't. She knew that. He'd warned her off. Caroline had warned her off. She could take a hint couldn't she? Tim hadn't wanted her, why should Steve Drake be any different? Why would any man want her? She held her breath waiting for him to go on, but it was obvious he'd said all he had to say as he turned on his heel and strode out.

4

All the way back to the medical centre, Steve was cursing himself. He'd done it again. Managed to get her back up with seemingly little effort. Why oh why, whenever he saw her, did this strange defence mechanism of his come into play? He couldn't even begin to explain it, except that every time he saw her, he had an impossible urge to kiss her and the only way to rid himself of such an urge, was either to annoy her or make fun of her.

Seeing her standing there, twiddling with the curtains, it was all he could do not to rush in behind her, grab her in his arms and swing her round. Then what? Kiss her? He wanted to, more than he cared to admit even to himself. If the truth were known, he'd wanted to from the very first moment he'd set eyes on her.

But there was absolutely no way he was ever going to let himself love another human being again. Ever.

★　★　★

At the end of her shift, Laura got into her car and it refused to start. 'Oh, terrific,' she mumbled. 'That's all I need.'

And to make matters worse, Steve Drake pulled into the car park and parked a few yards from her. 'Problems?' he asked as he climbed out and strolled over.

'I can't get it started,' she said. 'I think it's seized up in the cold.'

He frowned. 'It's not that cold. Let's have a look.' He tried to start it, then opened the bonnet and began to poke around in the engine.

'Are you sure you know what you're doing?' she asked nervously.

'When did you last have this serviced?' he asked, ignoring her question. 'You had a couple of loose leads and I've tightened them, but I think your starter motor is the problem.'

'Can you do anything about it?' she asked, rubbing her arms now as the chilly wind began to seep through to her bones.

'Yes,' he said, grinning as he straightened up. 'I'll call my mechanic and get him to take a look at it. In the meantime, you'll need a lift home.'

'I have to collect Abby from Claire's,' she said quickly. 'I can get a bus.'

'You'll do no such thing,' he told her firmly. As Laura saw it, she had no option. She got into his car and fastened her seat belt while he transferred Abby's carseat to his car.

'Now, where does this sister of yours live?'

'It's a long way out, Steve, I don't want to put you to all that trouble . . . '

'That's a strange address,' he chuckled softly.

She sighed and relaxed in the seat. 'She lives at Squirrel's Green in a house called Pooh Corner.'

'Pooh Corner?' he guffawed.

'I know, I know' Laura couldn't help grinning. 'She's always been mad about Winnie the Pooh.'

Steve drove out of the hospital car park and joined the main road heading out of town. He eventually pulled up outside Claire's big Victorian house, a great rambling family place. As they walked up the path, the big front door was flung open and Abby came hurtling out, straight into Laura's arms.

'Hello, darling,' Laura said, sweeping her up and planting a big kiss on her cheek. 'Have you been a good girl for Auntie Claire today?'

She didn't answer, but stretched her arms out towards Steve and instinctively he took her, hoisting her onto his wide shoulders.

'Looks like you've scored a hit there.' Claire said as she came out. 'It's Dr Drake, isn't it?'

Laura remembered her manners and carried out the introductions as they went inside the house.

'We've already met,' Claire remarked. 'You probably don't remember, but I saw you once several years ago when you first joined the practice.'

Steve grinned. 'You'd cut your finger opening a can of peaches and I stitched it for you,' he said. 'You're Dr Campbell's patient, but he was on holiday at the time.'

'What a memory,' Claire cried, clearly delighted he'd remembered her.

Claire's children were playing noisily and as usual, the place looked as if a tornado had swept through it. Within seconds, Steve was sitting cross legged on the floor with the children, a controller in his hands as Claire's oldest son explained how to operate the game on the screen. Laura could hardly believe her eyes. He looked so at home down there on the floor surrounded by children. Why on earth didn't he have kids of his own?

Claire made frantic eyes at Laura to follow her into the kitchen. When she did, Claire made a big thing of closing the door.

'What are you doing with him?' she hissed.

'My car broke down. He offered me a lift, that's all,' Laura said. 'So don't you go getting any romantic ideas — '

Claire's serious expression knocked the smile off her face. 'Romantic ideas — are you kidding?'

'Why? What is it, Claire?'

'He's not your new neighbour is he?' Claire asked in a concerned tone.

'The grumpy one,' Laura laughed. 'Yes, that's him.'

'Oh, Laura,' Claire groaned. 'You do pick them, don't you? I thought he'd moved out of the cottage after . . . well, a long time ago now. Surely you must know about — '

The door opened and Abby rushed in. 'Davey's been sick,' she announced. 'Steve says he's probably got the virus.'

'Oh, lord,' Claire said. 'That's all I need. It's been going round the school and I hoped this lot had managed to escape it. This means Abby will almost certainly catch it, too.'

'It's probably nothing to worry about,' Steve said, joining them in the kitchen. 'Would you like me to have a look at him while I'm here?'

'Oh, please,' Claire said.

Back in the sitting room he examined the little boy while Laura cleaned up the carpet. At last Steve stood up. 'Give him plenty to drink and if you're worried, call the health centre. He should be showing some signs of improvement within twenty-four hours.' He looked pointedly at his watch. 'We ought to be making tracks, Laura.'

Further explanations from Claire would have to wait, Laura decided as she hurried Abby into her coat and buttoned it up. She already had a good idea about what had happened in Steve Drake's past. There had been a woman in his life and there was no more. Presumably she'd walked out on him the way Tim had walked out on her.

She was still puzzling over this as he put Abby into the back seat and fastened her seat belt. 'Sit tight, princess,' he told her, then he opened the front passenger door for Laura.

Claire stood at the gate, her arms folded and a look of concern in her eyes before she waved them off.

Abby chatted non-stop all the way home, mainly to Steve who, to give him his due, was either genuinely interested or a jolly good actor.

When they pulled up outside the cottages, he turned to face Laura, his expression serious. 'Keep an eye on her, won't you. If she comes down with the virus, she's going to want her mum for a couple of days. They'll just have to manage at the unit without you.'

'Keep an eye on her?' Laura asked incredulously.

'I didn't mean . . . '

They got out of the car and while Abby bounded ahead looking as fit as the proverbial flea, Steve took Laura's arm and linked it through his.

'Stop taking everything I say the wrong way,' he whispered.

She knew she ought to draw away.

He was back to playing around with her emotions again and she shouldn't encourage him, but it felt so nice to be close to someone else — to be close to him — that she left it where it was. But when they reached her front door she had to extricate her arm from his.

'Thanks for the lift,' she said, feeling confused and not knowing what else to say to him.

'Is that it? I come to your rescue, and all you can say is thanks?'

'What do you want me to say?' she asked, perplexed.

'How about asking me in for a coffee?' he suggested.

Laura felt her heart begin to thud behind her ribs. It wouldn't hurt, would it? After all, he had gone out of his way to drive her all the way to Claire's.

With Steve sitting at the breakfast bar watching her every movement, Laura found her hands shaking. She missed the cup altogether with a spoonful of coffee and scattered it all over the work surface.

'Are you all right, Laura?'

'Of course I'm all right.' She deliberately moved away from him as he came round to stand beside her.

'Here, let me.' He took the spoon from her trembling fingers and finished making the coffee. 'Sit down, Laura.' She sank down on a stool and watched. 'Here.' He placed a cup in front of her. 'Think you can manage to drink it without spilling it all over the place, or shall I get you a bib?'

'Oh, very funny,' but she smiled to show she hadn't taken offence.

He didn't sit down with her, but walked to the window and watched as Abby wandered around in the garden, calling the wayward cat home.

'You've made it very nice in here,' he remarked. 'Very nice indeed.'

'I like it,' she said. And she did. She'd very carefully chosen summery yellows to decorate her home. Even on the darkest winter days, the cottage would look cheerful, bright and warm.

He turned back to look at her and it

was as if the breath had been knocked from him. He was almost reeling. While he'd been watching Abby, Laura had taken the pins from her hair letting it tumble freely about her shoulders in a riot of curls.

'You have very pretty eyes, Laura,' he said huskily. 'And you blush so beautifully,' he added with a grin. He was teasing her again.

'Have you finished your coffee, Steve?' she said, refusing to rise to the bait. 'I'd rather like to have an early night and — '

'All right,' he said, putting his cup down. 'I can take a hint.'

With a sigh of relief, she followed him to the door. He turned suddenly, unexpectedly and she almost walked into his chest.

'Say goodnight to Abby for me,' he said gruffly.

She looked up at him and felt the shaking begin all over again. This couldn't go on. She couldn't go around for the rest of her life behaving like a besotted teenager. If she couldn't pull herself together, then she'd have to leave Banford Mills for good.

'I'll say goodnight then,' he murmured.

'Goodnight, Doctor.'

For one terrible, heart stopping moment, she thought he was going to kiss her. If he does, I'll scream the place down, she thought frantically. I'll kick and punch and make him wish he'd never had the nerve. In the event, he simply smiled and turned away to open the door and when she closed it after him and leaned against it, it was disappointment not relief that flowed through her veins.

★ ★ ★

Steve stood for a moment staring at the door that had just been closed. Good God, he nearly kissed her — and he could just imagine how she would have reacted to that.

What was happening to him? Angry

with himself he spun round and stormed next door. He slammed into the cottage and went straight upstairs, stripping off and stepping into an ice cold shower. He'd either freeze to death or come to his senses, one or the other.

In the cottage next door, Laura was toying with the idea of calling Claire and asking what dark and dastardly secret lurked in Steve Drake's past — or maybe it was his present. But wouldn't that give away the fact that she was more than interested? She wasn't ready to share her thoughts or feelings with anyone just yet, not even her sister, and besides, whatever she felt for Steve Drake obviously wasn't going to be reciprocated.

'Can we have tea now, Mummy?' Abby asked. 'I'm starving.'

'Sure we can, sweetheart,' Laura said, jerking herself back to the here and now. 'You can set the table while I cook.'

Abby went off, happy to have something to do while Laura put a lasagne in the microwave to heat through. By the time she'd made a small salad, the lasagne was ready to eat. Abby had a hearty appetite, but then, she was always on the go, never still and probably burned tons of energy. Tim didn't know what he was missing. The thought struck Laura completely out of the blue and she realised she no longer cared that Tim might be missing out on seeing her grow up. Abby was fine. She was thriving, healthy and happy and that was all that mattered.

Tim had come to visit Abby at first, but she wasn't interesting enough for him and when she was six months old the visits stopped — and so did his maintenance payments. It hurt so much that he'd never wanted their little girl and had cast her adrift, never giving her a second thought.

'What's the matter?' Abby asked and Laura realised she'd been screwing her face up crossly. Immediately she smiled.

'Nothing, darling. I was just thinking about Auntie Claire, that's all. If

Davey's got that bug, she's going to have a lot to do just looking after him.'

'I'll help,' Abby announced.

She was very grown up for her age — too grown up. Laura didn't realise it until she compared her with other children of the same age. She talked like an adult most of the time and when they'd finished their meal, it was Abby who stacked the plates and carried them to the sink.

'Abby, I know you said you'd help Auntie Claire, but I really think it would be best if you didn't stay with her while Davey's ill.'

'That's all right,' Abby said, stuffing her tiny hands into huge rubber gloves. 'I can go to Mrs Gooding's house.'

Laura breathed a sigh of relief. Abby could have made things so difficult for her if she'd been of a mind. She stooped and hugged her daughter tight. 'Are you sure you don't mind, sweetheart? I'll have to give Mrs Gooding a ring to make sure it's okay.'

'Of course I don't mind, Mummy.'

Mrs Gooding was Mike's mother, a widow, who had looked after Claire's children and Abby when Claire and Mike had taken Laura out for a meal. She spent a lot of time at Claire's house and was not a stranger to Abby. It seemed the ideal solution.

'Leave the dishes,' Laura said, 'I'll sort them out later.'

Claire sounded relieved when Laura phoned to tell her she'd made alternative arrangements for Abby. She was happy too, because her mother-in-law lived quite close and Claire would be able to come to the rescue if there were any problems.

'Let's get you bathed and off to bed,' Laura said once everything was settled, and Abby nodded obediently and went towards the stairs. Abby was tired and drifted off to sleep as Laura read to her. Closing the book softly, Laura set it down then leaned over to give Abby a kiss.

'Don't grow up too quickly, darling,' she whispered.

She was such a lovely child, so angelic and yet there was a streak of mischief in her — like sending Steve up the tree to rescue Sam. Laura laughed softly and stroked the baby soft cheek before switching off the light and hurrying downstairs.

She'd discarded her uniform for a baggy grey track suit that was miles too big, but warm and comfortable and just right for rattling around the cottage and was about to start the washing up when the doorbell rang. Puzzled, she hurried to answer it.

'Steve,' she said. 'What are you doing here?' Her heart had given a tremendous leap at the sight of him, but that could have been relief for it was worrying to have callers at such a remote spot on a dark evening.

'I came to see you,' he said, smiling that gorgeous heart stopping smile that had all Laura's emotions running for cover. One more smile like that and she could very well be lost. He was leaning up against the door and in the shadows, his hair and eyes looked almost black. Most of all he looked devastatingly handsome.

'What did you want?' she asked defensively, afraid he might be able to see from the look on her face the way he was making her feel.

'Well you could invite me in and I'll tell you,' he suggested wryly.

'I was about to wash up,' she said stupidly.

He stepped into the hall and grinned. 'I'm an expert with a tea towel.'

Following her through to the kitchen, he said, 'Actually, I just called in to let you know about your car. It's been taken to the garage and should be ready for you by tomorrow afternoon. So I'll drive Abby to your sister's and you to the hospital in the morning.'

'There's no need . . . ' she began.

He grabbed a tea towel and began to dry up as she washed. 'Just being neighbourly,' he said with a shrug. 'I'm going to the medical centre to grab my correspondence, then I'm coming home. I have a week off.'

'Lucky you,' she smiled.

'I'm going to fix that fence,' he said as if he hadn't heard her. 'And I'm going to do something about the cottage. Seeing what you've done with your place here has inspired me.'

'I won't be taking Abby to my sister's tomorrow,' Laura said. 'She'll be staying with Claire's mother-in-law, just until things are back to normal at Claire's house.'

They washed up together, but all the time Laura's heart was going haywire inside her. It's no use letting your feelings get the better of you, she kept telling herself, you're just heading straight for heartache — but her emotions weren't listening.

'Would you like some coffee?' she asked.

'Love some,' he said, perfectly relaxed. 'I was right about your car, by the way — it was the starter motor.'

'Clever clogs.'

'I'm seldom wrong,' he said and for a

moment she thought he was being arrogant, then saw he was laughing and all the tension flooded out of her.

'Go and sit down,' she said. 'I'll bring the coffee through.'

When she came into the sitting room, he was sprawled in a chair, his long legs stretched out, his jeans taut around his muscular thighs. It was warm in the room and he'd pulled his sweater off leaving his hair tousled. She looked up, suddenly aware he was watching her appraisal of him, his mouth turned up at the corners and as she set the coffee down on the table, her hands shook so much that the cups rattled in their saucers. Flustered beyond belief, she sank trembling into an armchair, knowing her face must be glowing with embarrassment.

'Warm in here isn't it,' he remarked. 'Shall I turn the heater off?'

'Please,' she whispered, her voice a croak.

'What's wrong, Laura?'

'I don't know,' she said shakily. 'Just tired I guess.'

Tired — and confused about her feelings for Steve. And she'd been thinking a lot about Tim and the hurt of him leaving. She hadn't been hurt so much for herself, but for their little girl. How could a father not want anything to do with his own child? Tears sprang to her eyes and there was nothing she could do to hold them back. Blinded by tears, she didn't see him leave his chair and hurry over to her and didn't know he was there until she felt his arms close around her shaking body.

'Oh, love, don't cry,' he said tenderly.

She leaned against him, her tears soaking into his shirt feeling idiotic as her fists bunched up handfuls of his shirt.

'You don't know what you do to me,' he moaned softly, his lips brushing against her ear as he spoke. 'I'm not free to love you, Laura, I never will be . . . ' his voice cracked and broke and his arms tightened around her, then suddenly he was standing up, lifting her into his arms and then sinking back into the chair with her on his lap.

'Oh, love . . . ' he whispered. 'Don't cry, please don't cry.'

How long since she'd found comfort in a man's arms — in anyone's arms come to that? How many times had she so desperately needed a hug these past few years? Oh, there had been hugs galore from Abby, but they were different to this, so much different. And Tim had never been one for displays of affection. During their relationship, hugs had been rare.

What did Steve mean about not being free? Was there a Mrs Drake lurking somewhere in the background, or did someone just occupy such a huge space in his heart there simply wasn't room for anyone else? Frankly, at that moment, Laura couldn't have cared less.

This was her cuddle — her first in years — and she was going to make the most of it. It might be a few more years before it happened again. His hand moved to her hair, his fingers twining through the soft silky curls as he gently manoeuvred her head round so she was facing him. What he saw was a flushed, tear streaked face and eyes so huge and grey, vulnerable and trusting that his heart almost broke in two. Gently he kissed her long, thick lashes and tasted the salt of her tears, then slowly his lips moved down her face, kissing the tears from her cheeks until at last he reached her soft, trembling lips. She tightened her arms around his neck.

Then there was a piercing scream that had Laura scrambling from his lap.

'What the hell was that? Abby?' he cried.

'No — it came from outside,' Laura panted. And there it was again, a dreadful howling noise. 'It's Sam,' she said, frowning. 'There aren't any other cats around here, are there?'

'Mummy . . . ' Abby was rubbing her eyes, trailing a battered rag doll by its hair as she came into the room. 'What's that noise?'

How long had Sam been howling before they noticed, Laura wondered. She'd never forgive herself if anything happened to that cat.

'It's Sam, darling,' Laura said. 'He's probably trying to frighten something away. Steve's gone outside to see . . . '

And at that point, Steve returned, grinning all over his face, the cat floppy in his arms purring like mad as he tickled his ears. 'He was seeing off a fox,' he announced. 'He had the poor thing cornered . . . ' His voice was shaky, but he was laughing and gradually, as realisation dawned, Laura and Abby joined in. 'Here.' He bundled the cat into Laura's arms. 'You'd better feed him. I'll put Abby back to bed. Come on, princess.'

With that, he lifted the little girl over his shoulder and charged up the stairs. Abby's happy giggles drifted down to warm Laura's heart. That's what we both need, she thought, some warmth and love and laughter in our lives. And it would be so easy to fall in love with Steve . . .

He was back downstairs fairly quickly and Laura felt a tingle of anticipation. Would they take up where they left off? But anticipation turned to disappointment as he reached for his sweater, saying, 'I'd better go.'

'You don't have to . . . ' she said, her voice small as she prepared herself for rejection. She ought to be able to handle rejection by now.

'I do,' he replied and she could see the desire still smouldering in his eyes like a fire that refused to die. 'If I stay here with you, I won't be answerable for what happens.'

'Would that be so terrible?'

He wrapped his arms around her and held her close. 'Sleep on it, love,' he said gently. 'It wouldn't be terrible, but it might not be all that good for us. What we're feeling right now might not be all it seems. It may be that things are moving a little bit too quickly.'

He released her and made to go, but she called him back. 'Don't go . . .'

He turned and reached out, cupping her face in his hand and she covered his hand with hers. She wanted to tell him she was falling in love with him, but was afraid to say the words out loud, afraid he'd laugh at her.

She remembered the last time she'd said it to Tim. She really had loved him, but he'd flung it back in her face. 'If you loved me you would never have gone ahead and had that baby,' he had said.

'You don't mean that,' she'd whispered. 'You can't.'

'I do mean it,' he said.

Now Steve was talking to her again. 'Make sure you can cope with the flames before you light the fire,' he said.

Tears burned at her eyes and she dropped her head so he wouldn't see. The next she knew, the front door was closing and he'd gone and she felt more lost and alone than she'd ever felt in her life.

5

In the morning Steve drove Abby to Mrs Gooding's house, then went on to the hospital with Laura, but all the time, he hardly spoke, unless it was to talk to Abby. He looked tired, Laura thought, but then, so did she. She'd hardly slept at all with thoughts of Steve, the memory of his kiss, the pain of his rejection keeping her awake.

'Thanks for the lift,' she said coolly climbing out in the hospital car park.

'My pleasure,' he replied, not looking at her.

'You could have fooled me,' she muttered and then he looked up and there was a sudden glitter in his eyes as if they were full of ice crystals.

'Jim will bring your car here when it's ready. I told him to bring the keys to the Lodge.'

'Thanks,' she mumbled and hurried off.

She let herself into the Lodge and hurried down the corridor towards the office. Caroline Henderson emerged from one of the wards pushing the breakfast trolley and when she set eyes on Laura, she looked relieved.

'You're cutting it fine.' she said. 'I thought you'd got the dreaded bug.'

'Sorry,' Laura smiled. 'I've had problems with the car and Steve gave me a lift and . . . oh, it's a long story, Caroline.'

★   ★   ★

Last night had been a mistake, however real it had felt at the time. Steve was right about one thing, sleeping on it had given her a different perspective. Yet he'd said something about not being free. What had he meant by that? If only there was someone she could ask. She knew very well that if she asked questions of the nursing staff, conclusions would be leapt to and that's the last thing she wanted or needed right now. There was Claire of course, but she had enough on her hands with Davey being poorly.

Later, Laura was in her office with a young teenage girl, booking her in when there was a knock on her door. 'Yes?'

She drew in her breath sharply when Steve looked in and grinned at her.

'Sorry to butt in,' he said. 'Just letting you know I dropped Abby off okay. Ah, Tracey. Hi, there.'

'Hello, Doctor.'

'Tracey is your patient?' Laura asked.

'Certainly is, aren't you, love? Everything all right?'

'Yes, thanks,' Tracey grinned.

Laura had completely lost control of her heart. It was bouncing around behind her ribs like a ball in a squash court — or at least that's how it felt. The good talking to she'd given herself about the dangers of falling for a man like Steve hadn't worked at all.

'Well, you're in good hands with Sister Morgan,' he said and the praise created a shaft of pain so deep, she'd almost rather he'd said something awful about her.

'I thought you were supposed to be on holiday this week.'

'I am,' he protested. 'I'm just tying up a few loose ends.'

'Can't keep away, eh? It's no wonder you never get round to doing anything at the cottage.' Laura joked. 'Anyone would think you were finding excuses not to be there.'

He fixed her then with such a cold look that it made her stomach twist. She'd never seen anyone look so angry — or so hurt. What on earth had she said to put her foot in it now?

'See you later, Laura,' he said suddenly, then turning to Tracey his smile came back. 'And I'll see you at your next ante-natal appointment.'

'He's lovely isn't he?' Tracey whispered when he'd gone. 'You can't blame him though not wanting to stay at his house after what happened, though. It was him persuaded me to tell Dad about the baby. I wasn't going to. I was going to have an abortion. I thought it'd be easier than telling Dad.'

Laura shivered. How many girls had gone through abortion thinking it was the easy option? She wanted to rewind back to the bit about Steve, but now Tracey had started there was no stopping her.

'I thought Dad would shout and yell when I told him, so Dr Drake came round to the house and sat with me while I did it. Dad didn't shout or yell, or anything like that. The great soft lump just sat there and burst into tears. The only time I ever saw him cry before was when Mum died.'

'He obviously loves you a lot,' Laura said hoarsely. Her throat was tight and she almost felt like crying. But her tears would have been for herself because the way Steve Drake had glared at her had cut her to the quick.

But Tracey's words kept coming back to her. 'You can't blame him not wanting to stay at his house after what happened.' What did happen? It certainly wouldn't be right to ask Tracey to explain.

'Right,' she said breezily. 'Let's finish off getting this form filled in.'

★ ★ ★

The rest of the day was fairly quiet until at three o'clock in the afternoon, the mechanic delivered her car and handed Laura the keys.

'Thank you,' she said gratefully. 'You don't know how pleased I am to have my car back. How much do I owe you?'

'Dr Drake settled up,' he said and her heart sank. That meant she would have to now go and thank him and pay him back. And she was hoping not to have to see him.

Worse was to come. When she arrived to collect Abby, it was a haggard looking Mike who came to the door.

'Mike,' she cried in surprise. 'What are you doing here?'

'It's Mum,' he said. 'She's got this

virus now. Davey's just getting over it, but Sian's running a temperature and complaining of tummy ache, and I think Claire's got it as well. I'm taking Mum back to our house until she's feeling better.'

'Oh, Mike, I am sorry,' Laura said. 'Is there anything I can do? Anything I can get for you?'

'No, I don't think so. Look, I'm sorry Laura, but there's no way Claire or Mum can look after Abby tomorrow. I'm really sorry, but . . . '

'Of course there's no question of you having to look after Abby,' she said. 'I'll be able to make alternative arrangements. The important thing right now is that you and the family take care of yourselves.'

Though God only knew what arrangements could be made. Laura didn't relish the idea of leaving her with a stranger, yet what else could she do? She could hardly take time off when they were already so short staffed.

'Don't worry about it, Mike. I'll just

pop in and see Claire before I go.'

She left Mike to get his mother ready to be moved and went to her sister's house. Claire was in bed with Sian, but Davey seemed fine now.

'I feel awful,' Claire moaned. 'I've never been so sick in all my life. I wish I hadn't got on to Davey for making such a fuss now. If he was feeling half as bad as me . . .'

'Poor thing,' Laura said. 'If there's anything I can do, let me know.'

'Oh, Mike's got everything under control,' Claire said.

'Just don't let yourself get dehydrated — drink lots,' Laura reminded her.

'Yes, nurse, whatever you say.' Claire pulled a face and Laura laughed. Then Claire became serious. 'What about Abby? Can you get time off to look after her? You don't want to send her to a stranger. She's been hassled enough this week.'

'That's my problem,' Laura said firmly. 'Let someone else do the worrying for a change and you just concentrate on getting better, okay?'

'Okay,' Claire conceded. 'But promise you won't leave Abby with a stranger. She might appear all grown up and confident on the outside, but she's just a little tot underneath.'

'I know that,' Laura said. 'She is my daughter.'

'And you're my little sister,' Claire chuckled and then croaked, 'And I still treat you like a kid, don't I?'

Laura leaned over the bed and kissed Claire on the forehead. 'Take care,' she said. 'And make the most of the rest.'

Claire beckoned her back. 'About Steve — I was going to tell you . . . '

She was burning to know, but Claire wasn't well and she was afraid that if they got into a conversation about Steve, her feelings would be as plain as the nose on her face. She'd never been able to fool Claire and now wasn't the time to try. 'Tell me some other time,' she said. 'When you're better.'

Claire slumped back against the

pillows with a groan of protest. 'Just be careful,' she warned. 'Watch yourself, sis. Steve Drake is a heartache waiting to happen.'

Don't I know it, Laura thought.

★ ★ ★

Gripping Abby's hand tightly and taking a deep breath, Laura knocked on Steve Drake's door. After what felt like an age, he answered it dressed casually in jeans and a white shirt. His hair was damp from a shower and moisture still trickled down his neck. Laura watched a drop trail all the way down into the open neck of his shirt, before she jolted herself, looked up at him and found he was looking down at her with that odd mixture of sadness and amusement in his eyes.

'Hello, Laura. Hi, Abby. What can I do for you?'

'I've come to pay you,' she mumbled, opening her bag.

'Mrs Gooding's sick now, too,' Abby

announced. 'She was in the bathroom for hours.'

'Aw, I'm sorry to hear that, princess,' Steve said sympathetically.

'Uncle Mike had to come and look after her,' Abby continued.

'Uncle Mike?'

Laura noticed his eyes darken at the mention of Mike's name. She thought it was time she put the record straight. 'My brother-in-law,' she said. 'Claire's husband. How much was the garage bill — and would you mind if I give you a cheque?'

'Laura, forget the bill for a minute will you? How's Davey?'

'He's getting better,' Abby informed him, determined to monopolise the conversation. 'Sian's not well either and — '

'That's enough, Abby,' Laura interrupted. 'If I could just pay you . . . '

'Come in,' he said, then when she just stood there unmoving, he said impatiently, 'Come in, Laura. You're letting the cold in. I've got a copy of the bill somewhere — I'll give it to you.'

Laura had a shock when she walked into his sitting room. The furniture was covered in dust sheets and the walls were half stripped of paper. 'I see you've made a start on the decorating.'

'I don't even know what I'm putting in its place yet,' he admitted ruefully. 'I always left that sort of thing to — ' He broke off and closed his eyes and Laura held her breath waiting for him to continue. Who, she wanted to ask; who did you always leave it to? Did she walk out on you like Tim walked out on me? Is that why you're not free, because you're waiting for her to come back? Damn her, whoever she is for hurting you so much!

'Blue,' Laura said, hoping to salvage something for him.

'Blue?' He opened his eyes and looked at her.

'Mmmm,' she nodded. 'Dusky blue, maybe Wedgwood. With a border to break up the colour. I think that would go very nicely in this room.'

'Maybe I should ask your advice before I go ahead and buy anything,' he said and handed her a sheet of paper. 'Your bill.'

It wasn't as much as she'd been expecting and she quickly wrote a cheque and handed it to him.

'Thanks,' he said, poking it into the breast pocket of his shirt. 'Wasn't too much of a shock, was it? I usually find he charges a pretty reasonable rate and does a good job.'

'No complaints,' she said. 'Thanks again, Steve. Come on, poppet. I have to make a few calls, to try to find a temporary child minder for you.'

They were at the door by now and Abby had stepped outside. 'There's Sam. He's waiting on the doorstep for us.' Abby cried and took off.

'You're not serious,' Steve said as Laura made to follow. 'About leaving her with a complete stranger I mean?'

'I don't have any choice, and it is only a temporary arrangement until Claire's on her feet again,' Laura said, bristling. 'It's all right for people like you to be judgemental, but you don't have any ties and you wouldn't know the first thing about having to arrange your life around a child's needs.'

He flinched. 'What if she's ill?' he said.

'Well, what do you suggest, Steve?' Laura cried. 'What other option do I have? I can't just not turn up at the Lodge when we're already short staffed, I can't take her with me and I certainly can't leave her here on her own.'

'Then leave her with me,' he said. 'She knows me, you know me. I do know a bit about kids, you know.'

'I'm sure you do, but taking care of a lively little girl is a lot different to tending to sick children,' she said. 'And what do you know about — '

The look on his face froze her mid-sentence.

'Think it over and let me know what you decide in the morning,' he said coldly, then he closed the door and she was left standing on the doorstep feeling utterly bereft.

6

Standing in the centre of the room, surrounded by shreds of wallpaper, Steve glared at the bare walls. He wished he'd never started this now, never got involved with Laura. Too late for that, a little voice inside his head mocked him. Like it or not, you are involved. He laughed raggedly, remembering her explanation about Uncle Mike. If he'd known before that the guy was just her brother-in-law, would it have made any difference? Most probably, he decided. But it was too late now for ifs and buts.

He couldn't be falling in love with Laura Morgan. It was impossible. Once he'd loved Tricia with all his heart, with every fibre of his being as the saying went. Laura was so different to his wife. Tricia had been tall, slender and strikingly attractive while Laura was petite and dark and beautiful. They were different in personality, too. Tricia was outgoing and exuberant, a real extrovert, yet Laura was quiet and gentle. So why compare them?

And why did he feel so guilty?

Maybe because it was his fault that Tricia and Lucy were dead. The thought struck him with the force of a blow and he reeled back, throwing the wallpaper scraper into a bucket of soapy water. His thoughtlessness, his alone, had led to the deaths of his wife and child and if he was suffering punishment and torment now, it wasn't because of grief, but guilt.

* * *

The following morning, Laura tapped tentatively on Steve's door, then looked down at Abby who was smiling happily, looking forward to spending the day with Steve. When he opened the door, she gasped. He looked dreadful, as if he hadn't slept a wink either. His eyes were red rimmed, but they still lit up slightly at the sight of them standing there.

'If the offer's still open . . . ' she began.

'Of course it is,' he said. He scooped Abby up into his arms and she giggled and wriggled with delight.

'She'll be fine with me, won't you, princess?' he said happily. 'Even if I am a last resort.'

'I'll see you later, poppet,' Laura said, ruffling Abby's golden curls and kissing her. 'Be good for Steve, won't you?'

'I will,' Abby tightened her arms around Steve's neck.

Laura hurried down to the gate and then stopped and turned to look at them. Abby looked so tiny and yet so safe in Steve's muscular arms.

Oddly enough, it hadn't been thoughts of Steve Drake that had disturbed her sleep last night, but memories of her marriage to Tim. Theirs had been a passionate, whirlwind romance. She'd been so sure of him, so certain of their love that when he asked her to marry him, she hadn't even hesitated in giving him her answer. They were married quickly — and happily — and it wasn't until Laura became pregnant that the huge differences between them became obvious.

'You can't have a baby,' Tim had said, horrified.

'What do you mean, can't have a baby?' she'd asked, trembling.

'Exactly what I say. I don't want children.' He couldn't cope with the broken nights, however hard Laura tried to make sure he wasn't disturbed. He hated his home being cluttered with baby paraphernalia and after sticking it for almost a month, he'd packed up and left.

Maybe if she'd done as he'd wanted and gone through with an abortion, they might still be together, but she doubted it. She hoped that once the baby was born, he might have a change of heart, but there was simply nothing there and her love for him had finally died. It had left her with scars. She was so frightened of being hurt again, not just for herself, for Abby too.

By the time she drove into the hospital, she was feeling sorry for herself and made a conscious effort to cheer up as she walked into the Lodge. She told Caroline about her problems finding a child minder for Abby at short notice — and who had stepped into the breach.

'Steve?' Caroline gasped and looked so shocked that alarm bells began to clang in Laura's head.

'What's wrong with that?' Laura asked nervously.

'Wrong with it?' Caroline replied. 'There's nothing wrong with it. It's just . . . well, for a start when Steve Drake takes a holiday, he still manages to visit the health centre or the hospital every day, you know what I mean? He's . . . well, I think he's lonely. People tend to forget what happened because it was so long ago, but I don't think he's ever really gotten over it, or that he ever will.' With a shake of her head, she stood up and put her coffee cup down, but Laura pulled her round to face her.

'Over what, Caroline?' she asked, her face pale, her grey eyes intense. 'What hasn't Steve Drake ever gotten over?' Her heart was thudding painfully. She was about to find out Steve's secret, the reason perhaps that he wasn't free to love her.

'Don't you know?' Caroline whispered.

'Of course I don't know,' Laura said. 'No one ever gossips about him — except to warn me to keep away from him.'

Caroline bit her lip and regarded Laura steadily for a moment or two as if considering whether to tell. In the end, she gave a heavy sigh. 'It's no secret and I don't suppose he'll mind if I tell you. I dare say he assumes you already know.'

'Just tell me, Caroline. If this is likely to affect my daughter's safety . . . '

'Oh, no.' Caroline cried. 'You mustn't

think that. He adores children and — look at the time — I'll have to tell you all about it later, okay?'

Laura had to agree, what other choice did she have? They were rushed off their feet.

★ ★ ★

The afternoon was taken up with mundane, almost trivial matters. No sooner had Laura managed to get one thing out of the way, than something else cropped up. When she did have a quiet few minutes, her fingers itched to pick up the phone and call Steve, but the thought of his reaction put her off. Then, when things were winding down towards the end of Laura's shift, a young woman arrived with her mother. She was in early labour, but her worried mother had brought her in.

Laura settled them in, but knew the baby wouldn't be born during her shift, unless it happened tomorrow when she came back on duty. It simply meant the last few minutes were eaten up and when she finally handed over to the night sister, Caroline had already gone.

The cottages were in darkness when Laura finally arrived home and she felt a tremor of dread crawl under her skin. Had something happened? Fear brought her out in a cold sweat. If anything happened to Abby . . . but Steve wouldn't let anything happen to her, she told herself firmly. She trusted him implicitly, otherwise she wouldn't have left Abby with him in the first place. She'd simply been unsettled by Caroline's suggestion that something was not quite right.

Afterwards she didn't know why she did what she did but, instead of going in by the front door of the cottage, she walked around to the back garden. Steve and Abby were in his garden squatting close to the house. As she moved towards the fence, she saw too late that they were watching a fox. She was surprised at how small it was — not much bigger than a cat — and rather ragged looking. For a moment woman and fox stared at each other in the moonlight, then the fox turned suddenly and vanished.

'Oh, Mummy.' Abby cried. 'Did you see her? We put some food out and she came to eat it.'

'You fed the fox?' Laura asked in disbelief.

Steve straightened up and shrugged. 'She's hungry. You saw how thin she was. I gave her some of Sam's cat food. Pilchard flavour,' he mumbled.

Laura laughed. He looked and sounded as if he expected a ticking off, but that was the last thing on Laura's mind. She was swamped with relief at seeing Abby safe and sound and further swamped with something else at the sight of Steve, something she couldn't put a name to but felt very nice.

She'd been worried about him, too, but she didn't know why.

'You gave the fox Sam's favourite food.' Laura laughed out loud. 'He'll never forgive you, you know.'

'Talking of food, there's pizza and baked potatoes in the oven,' he said.

'You didn't have to bother,' Laura began and he sighed.

'It was no bother, Laura.' Then turning to Abby, he said, 'Go in and put on the lights, princess.'

'Have I time to get changed?' Laura asked.

'Ten minutes,' he said and she turned and rushed into her own cottage.

What to wear. Anyone would think she was going on an important first date instead of just next door for a pizza. She flung open her wardrobe doors and rummaged, finally choosing a long silky skirt and a plain white top with a lace edging. Simple, but feminine. She had a very quick wash, put on a little make up and hurried next door.

Steve stared at her standing in the doorway. The long navy skirt with tiny white flowers swirled nearly to her trim ankles and the plain white top clung provocatively to her slim figure. She'd let her hair down, like it was on that first day, softly surrrounding her face in a riot of wild tendrils. It was a very simple outfit, but on her it looked stunning. But more than anything else it was the look on her face that set his heart racing, the wide-open set of her eyes, so trusting, so vulnerable, the black sweep of her lashes. Her lips full and slightly parted and with them came the memory of that kiss. She'd tasted every bit as sweet as he'd expected. Even the memory of it stirred him more than he would have thought possible.

'Did you have a busy day?'

'Was Abby any trouble?'

They both spoke at once, then broke off, laughing in embarrassment as they made frantic signals to each other to be the first to speak. And then, in the confusion, they both began to speak again.

'I'll answer your question first,' he said at last. 'No, Abby wasn't any trouble. She was a delight to have around and she helped me choose some blue paint for the sitting room,' he added, somewhat sheepishly. 'More or less Wedgwood with a scroll border and curtain fabric to match.'

'You have been busy,' she said, pleased that he'd taken her advice.

'I'm having the curtains made, so they'll be ready by the time I've finished the painting . . . Hell, Laura, why are we wasting time talking about curtains?'

Her heart skipped a beat. 'Would you rather talk about something else?'

'You,' he answered simply.

'Me?' she almost choked and then Abby came in and rescued her.

'I laid the table, Mummy — look! I've had a wonderful day,' she announced, hunched up her shoulders and gave a delicious little shiver.

'Me too,' Steve added, then turned away and opened the oven door.

The meal was delicious — and very filling. It was nice to be able to relax and take her time. Steve and Abby chatted happily, telling her all about their day. Listening to the pair of them warmed her heart and at the same time brought it home to her how much Abby missed not having a father.

When they washed up, Steve sent Abby off to the sitting room to watch a Disney film on the video. 'Does she ever stop talking?' He laughed.

'Would you believe she didn't utter a single word until she was three years old?' Laura said. 'I was worried sick about her and my GP was about to send her for all sorts of tests when she suddenly started. It wasn't just the odd word here and there but lengthy sentences, long words and phrases. It's as if she'd spent all that time storing up information and didn't let any of it out until she was ready.'

'She's a very bright girl,' he said, plunging his hands into the soapy water and bringing out a plate. 'She's got an amazing vocabulary. And did you know that Einstein didn't say a word until he was three either?'

'Ah, so my daughter is a budding genius!' He passed her the plate and, as she took it, her hand brushed against his. 'What are we going to do, Steve?' she whispered. 'We can't go on like this.'

'No,' he said. 'You're right, this is silly. I want you, Laura. I want you like crazy. But . . . you've been married before,' he said. 'So have I. Is your ex-husband . . . I mean, did he hurt you very much?'

'Tim?' she said. 'I was upset when he walked out — angry — but the hurt was more for Abby. You have to love someone before they can hurt you.'

'You didn't love your husband?' He looked horrified. 'Why did you marry him? Why have his child?'

'I thought I loved him at the time.'

'And he walked out on you?' Steve asked.

'What did you think? That I was the one who threw my marriage away?'

'No. I hadn't really thought about it.'

'I never told anyone this, Steve' she whispered. 'And Abby must never find out . . . Tim didn't want children.'

'You mean he let your marriage break up because of Abby?' Steve gasped incredulously. 'He threw you and that lovely little girl away? What a damned fool he must have been!'

He was suddenly distant. He was hiding something, some dark, sad secret. If only she knew what it was, maybe she could help. Dare she ask him? 'Steve . . . ?'

He shook his head. 'It couldn't work with us, Laura,' he said. 'I don't think I'll ever be ready to make a commitment to another person again and I don't think you . . . '

The reasoning behind his words began to sink in — and it hurt. Hurt more than she would have thought possible. It was a real physical pain deep down inside, as if he'd thrust a knife into her gut and twisted. Throwing her usual caution to the wind, she murmured, 'I'm willing to try.'

'No, you don't understand. You've been there, you know how you can be fooled into thinking you love someone only to find you've made a dreadful mistake.'

'Yes, I made a mistake,' she said. 'One mistake. I was young and — oh, why am I even bothering to try and explain to you? It's clear you don't even want to listen. You're so wrapped up in yourself, in your own heartbreak whether it's real or imagined . . . ' She wished she knew the right thing to say. 'You can't spend the rest of your life punishing yourself,' she said at last, trying to choose her words carefully. 'Unless you enjoy making a martyr of yourself. Is that it, Steve?'

'I think you'd better go now, Laura,' he said and his voice was as cold as ice, so cold it chilled her to the bone.

'You've got to stop running some time,' she said. 'Face up to what happened and try and forget . . . '

'Forget?' There was no ice now as his eyes blazed with fire. 'Forget? How can I ever forget? How could you even suggest I try?'

It would have helped if she'd known

what she was talking about, if she'd waited to find out before speaking her mind, for it was clear she'd put her foot in it — both feet probably. 'I'm sorry,' she mumbled, utterly mortified that she'd wounded him so deeply.

'Just go, Laura, please. Just go.'

Numb with shock, she hurried to the sitting room and pulled Abby to her feet. 'Come along, we're going home,' she said abruptly.

'But I'm watching . . . '

Steve came into the room behind them and switched off the video. 'You can watch the rest tomorrow,' he told her.

Laura took a deep breath. 'You still want me to bring her round?'

'Why not? It isn't her fault her mother's — '

Laura closed her eyes, preparing herself for a hurtful assault, but none came. When she opened her eyes he was simply looking at her, his own eyes filled with despair. He looked wounded, torn and again she had to stifle the urge to hold him.

'I'll be a little later tomorrow,' she said, swallowing her despair like a bitter pill. 'I'm not due at the Lodge until eleven.'

'Whenever,' he said casually. 'I'll be here.'

'Night, night, Steve,' Abby said, lifting her arms up to him.

His whole body sagged, his expression softening and Laura felt a stab of pain. If only he'd look at her like that, accept her love as readily as he accepted Abby's.

7

The following morning dawned quite beautiful, mellow and golden, and when Laura opened the curtains it was to see little brown rabbits soaking up the sunshine. Through the trees, the river looked incredibly blue, the prettiest colour she'd seen it since she'd moved into the cottage.

She got Abby out of bed, dressed her warmly in a red sweater and jeans and gave her breakfast.

'We'll go for a walk before I go to work,' she said. 'We haven't been along the river bank yet and it's a lovely day.'

'But, Mummy, Steve says I must stay away from the river,' Abby replied. 'He says it's dangerous.'

Suppressing her sudden irritation, Laura said, 'Well, it's all right so long as you're with me.'

Even so, Abby took some persuading

and Laura was left to wonder what on earth Steve had said to instil such fear in her daughter's mind.

The way was muddy, but once they reached the path that ran alongside the river, the ground was drier. It must be safe to walk along here, Laura told herself. After all, lots of people came past the cottage with their dogs. She'd even seen children trooping down with fishing rods and canvas bags. There was no question of Steve dashing out and warning them off, so why did he feel it necessary to do it to her?

They'd walked quite some distance when she saw a small wooden jetty jutting into the river. The tide was almost in, but there was a sandy strip between the water and the bank. Laura sat down on a tree stump and looked around. It was a lovely view from here across the river to the other side. It was an ideal spot for summer picnics and long walks on balmy summer evenings.

'Can I walk out there?' Abby asked, pointing to the end of the jetty.

'I don't see why not,' Laura agreed. 'Just make sure you keep well away from the edge and don't go to the very end.'

She watched, smiling as Abby carefully walked out on the jetty. At one point she knelt down and peeped through the boards at the water below. How wonderful to be a child, to have all of life in front of you and everything an adventure, Laura thought. It was going to be great here in the summer. Perhaps they could hire a boat and go sailing.

A jet plane suddenly roared overhead and Abby jumped to her feet and looked up, shielding her eyes against the sun. She spun round, almost lost her footing, stumbled . . .

Laura was already starting to her feet when she heard a shout. Abby was all right, standing steady again, still a safe distance from the edge, but she could hear footsteps pounding along the river path towards them.

Sheltered from view by brambles and ivy and a dozen other plants that thrived in the moist atmosphere close to the river, Laura watched in horror as Steve appeared, his face a mask of terror. She'd never seen anyone look as frightened as he did in that moment.

'Abby,' he shouted, starting along the jetty. 'Abby, stand still, love. Stay right where you are.'

Abby looked frightened too. Laura saw her little mouth turn down, her eyes well with tears as she put her arms up to Steve. He fell to his knees beside her, wrapping her in his arms.

Laura came to her senses then and ran from cover, along the jetty. What in the name of God was he thinking of, frightening Abby like that? What was it all for? The child's frightened sobs rent the air as she clung tightly to Steve's neck. Laura stopped just short of them, an angry rebuke dying in her throat. He was still holding Abby as if he'd never let her go and she was clinging to him and when he looked up at Laura, she was shocked at the sight of tears wet on his cheeks.

The last of her anger just evaporated. 'Oh, Steve,' she said. 'What is it — whatever is it?'

Slowly he got to his feet, taking Abby with him. 'I told you to keep away from the river,' he blazed, his anger like a slap in the face. 'Both of you. What were you doing here?'

She backed away, stunned at the change in him. 'We came for a walk, that's all. Abby was quite safe — I was watching from over there. If anything happened, I could have been with her in seconds,' she stammered.

'You fool,' he said scathingly. 'I told you about the river. It's unpredictable and deadly. It looks pretty on a day like this, but underneath that sparkling water there are strong currents.'

'I can swim, Steve,' she said softly. 'And so can Abby.'

But he wasn't listening, he was striding back towards the cottages, still clutching Abby in his arms. Anyone would think she was his child the way he was carrying on. Laura held her anger in check until they were back home and Abby was sitting on the floor in front of the television watching the video she'd started to watch the night before.

Then she let it go. 'I don't know what hang ups you've got about that river,' she hissed furiously, 'but whatever they are, don't try to put them on me and Abby. I won't have her frightened like that. Did you see her little face? She was terrified — and for no good reason.'

She waited for his angry retort, but it was as if all the rage had gone out of him leaving behind an empty shell.

'I'm sorry,' he said softly. 'I wouldn't have frightened her for the world — or you. I just . . . I saw her standing out there on the jetty and I thought she was alone, then that jet went over . . . ' he broke off and pressed his fingers into his face. 'It made her jump. I thought she was going to fall. I thought . . . '

'You know I wouldn't have let her go down there on her own and besides, she knows she's not to. I had a difficult enough job persuading her to come with me. But people go down there every day, I see them walking past the cottage.'

'Shouldn't you be getting ready for work?' he asked abruptly and she was taken aback by the sudden about-turn in his attitude. A moment ago he'd been lost, helpless, now he was acting gruffly again.

'Yes, I hadn't realised how late it was getting. Will you be all right?'

'I'll be fine,' he said. 'I over reacted, that's all. Has anyone spoken to you yet about the proposed changes in our antenatal care?'

'What?' Laura was stunned at this sudden change in the direction of the conversation. He was no longer an unhappy, hurting man, but a doctor, the calm professional.

'It's nothing major,' he said. 'Just that at our antenatal clinic at the health centre, we'd like to have a midwife present rather than the practice nurse.

As it stands, it's only the women who come to the classes who get to meet the midwives.'

'Oh, that,' Laura nodded. 'Yes, I spoke to Dr Wilson about it yesterday. Caroline's going to attend — '

'No,' he said. 'Not at my clinic. I want you, Laura.'

'But, I . . . '

'It's only one afternoon a week and you're just five minutes away from the Lodge if an emergency crops up.'

'Why me?'

He smiled but didn't give her an answer. He couldn't — he didn't have an answer, not one he found acceptable anyway.

'I'd better go,' she said, her thoughts once again thrown into utter confusion. 'I'll just say goodbye to Abby.'

* * *

Caroline looked at Laura across the top of her coffee cup and said, 'I can't believe you haven't been told about it.'

'Then tell me about it, Caroline — and before something happens and I have to rush off.'

'Steve was married to Tricia. She was a model, very beautiful. They had a strange kind of marriage. She'd go off on these modelling assignments all over the place, often abroad to really exotic locations. He worshipped her, absolutely adored her.'

Why did that hurt, Laura wondered, the thought that he'd once loved someone else so much? She'd loved Tim once — or she thought she did.

'She wanted him to give up being a doctor and go with her, but he wouldn't do that. Instead he bought the cottage down by the river and got himself a boat. When she was abroad, he'd go sailing, when she was home they'd usually go to stay in London so she could be near the bright lights. She loathed it here, absolutely hated it.'

Laura frowned. It seemed a very odd relationship.

'He did everything he could to keep

her. He even had interior decorators in to do up the cottage so it looked like something out of a glossy magazine, exactly as she wanted it. Then she fell pregnant. She gave up modelling for a while and we all thought she'd settle down, but she started getting restless.'

Caroline stopped to finish her coffee. She looked uncomfortable and Laura now understood why no one gossiped about Steve. This went beyond normal hospital gossip. This was serious stuff and Caroline obviously wasn't happy recounting it.

'The baby,' Laura asked hoarsely. 'Was it a little girl?'

'Lucy, yes. She was the spitting image of Tricia, the absolute double. By the time she was toddling, they were both being snapped up for assignments. Steve hated it. He wanted Lucy to have a normal childhood. The last straw for him was coming in one day to find strangers swarming all over his house and Lucy sitting there with heated rollers in her hair crying her poor little heart out. He flipped and ordered them all out.'

'Caroline, how do you know all this?' Laura asked. 'How much of it is just pure conjecture?'

Caroline's face twisted with pain. 'I knew Tricia quite well. She told me things. Anyway, they had this almighty row, but agreed to have one last try for Lucy's sake.'

Laura felt a wave of dizziness wash over her. She had a horrible feeling she knew what was coming, but her mind fought against it. No, she thought, no it couldn't possibly be . . .

'He came home from the hospital one afternoon. It was spring, there'd been an extra high tide.' Tears filled Caroline's eyes. 'He adored that little girl, absolutely doted on her and of course, she loved him. I think she was closer to Steve than she was to her mother. If she was hurt or ill, it was always him she wanted.'

'What happened, Caroline?' Laura whispered.

'I'm sorry. It always upsets me to talk about it . . . Lucy was my godchild.'

Laura reached across and held Caroline's hand.

'Steve got home one day and found the lane full of police and ambulances. They'd drowned in the river, Laura, both of them.'

'Oh Caroline,' Laura said, rubbing at her eyes. No wonder Steve had blown up at her just this morning for letting Abby play on the jetty. And no wonder he didn't want any kind of a relationship with her.

'The last thing Steve would want would be your pity or your sympathy,' Caroline said. 'But as far as his personal life goes, he's cut himself off these last few years. It's almost as if he'd blocked out what happened.'

'And when Abby and I moved in next door, we brought it all back,' Laura said, suddenly understanding.

'Yes, Abby,' Caroline said. 'Perhaps he sees in her a replacement for the child he lost.'

It explained so much. While Laura was falling in love with him, thinking that somewhere deep down, he felt the same, all the time it was Abby he wanted, a child to replace his daughter.

Oh, she should have known shouldn't she? If she'd been any use at all, wouldn't Tim have made more of an effort to hold their marriage together? She pushed thoughts of Tim away. He'd been utterly selfish, not wanting children because they might cramp his lifestyle. In a million years, Steve couldn't be like that.

'How old was she? How old was Lucy when . . . when she died?'

'Three, almost four,' Caroline said. 'Now do you see what it is I'm trying to tell you?'

'Oh, Caroline,' she breathed as the enormity of it all began to sink in. 'What am I going to do?'

Caroline reached out and squeezed Laura's hand. 'I don't know, love.'

And then it came to her, all those things she'd said, thoughtless words she wouldn't have dreamed of speaking had she known the root cause of his heartache. He must think she was a heartless bitch.

★ ★ ★

While Laura was learning the truth about Lucy and Tricia and the whole tragic accident, Steve was sitting sprawled in an armchair with Abby nestling in his arms as he read to her from a book. It was only when she felt extremely heavy that he realised she'd fallen asleep.

'Was I that boring?' he whispered, dropping a kiss on top of her head. Asleep, she was like a little doll and it amazed Steve just how much she'd come to mean to him in such a short time. He didn't think it was possible he could ever love another child.

He thought about what had almost happened that morning and a shudder went through him. It had brought back that day so clearly. He'd come home a little late and had stopped off on the way to pick up flowers for Tricia. They were lying on the back seat and the car was filled with their heady perfume. Even then, even when it was obvious the marriage was dead, he was still trying desperately to salvage something from the wreckage, to make it work, if only for Lucy's sake. Driving down the bumpy track, he'd seen the flashing of a blue light through the trees and when he turned the corner he saw the ambulance and police cars parked outside the cottages and knew something terrible had happened.

He remembered getting out of the car and could almost feel the sudden terrible silence that greeted his arrival.

'Dr Drake? We've been trying to get hold of you, sir. Would you like to come inside . . . ?'

Someone tried to lead him into his cottage. Then he noticed the stranger, a good looking young guy with jet black hair who was sitting in the police car, his feet on the ground, tears running down his face. Steve could see him now in his mind's eye as clearly as if he were right here in front of him. He was one of Tricia's crowd, one of the many hangers-on who always seemed to fill the cottage. He had walked slowly to the man sitting in the car. Now he was reliving that moment when he came face to face with his wife's lover.

'What happened?' he'd rasped.

'It wasn't my fault,' the young man bleated, fresh tears tumbling down his face. 'It wasn't my fault.'

And then Steve had hold of him, bunching up the front of his jacket in his fists, hauling him bodily from the car and shaking him. 'What happened, damn you! Where's Lucy? Where is she?' And then they were coming along the path carrying a body wrapped from head to toe. 'No!' he screamed, letting the young man go. 'No! For God's sake! Lucy!'

But it wasn't Lucy, it was Tricia. Lucy's body didn't turn up until several agonising days later.

'Lucy,' he whispered softly, sadly. 'Oh, Lucy.'

In his arms, Abby began to stir. No wonder. He was wound up as tight as a drum. 'Who's Lucy?' she asked sleepily, and the innocence of her question cut him like a knife.

He must have called out Lucy's name without even realising it. Oh, God, would it ever stop hurting? It was his fault, all his fault. If he hadn't stifled Tricia, hadn't tried to mould her into his idea of a wife and mother, none of it would have happened, Lucy would still be alive.

'Lucy was my daughter,' he replied and Abby stroked his hand.

'Did she go away? Like my daddy?'

Wordlessly, he nodded and she put her little arms around his neck and rested her face against his chest. 'Will you finish the story now?' she asked and he laughed softly.

'Yes, princess. Now where were we . . . ?'

* ★ ★

Laura hurried home that evening, more anxious to get back than usual. Now she knew, it had changed everything.

No sooner had she parked her car than Steve was coming towards her, holding tight to Abby's hand. Her heart gave a painful lurch at the sight.

Abby tugged her hand free and ran into Laura's arms. 'Hello, Mummy. I've been helping Steve to paint — come and see what we've done.'

Laura picked her up and buried her face in Abby's soft hair. She'd never been so pleased to see her. She had a sudden vision of her out on that jetty and imagined what must have gone through Steve's mind when he saw her.

It must have brought it all rushing back. It must be hell having to live with that day in, day out.

'I don't think there's time,' Steve said when Laura hesitated. 'You'll be wanting to get home for your tea.'

So there was to be no meal waiting

for her tonight, Laura thought ruefully. Still, what else did she expect? All the time he'd been fighting his feelings, trying to warn her, she'd been rushing blindly in, naively hoping to make him change his mind.

'Oh, I think I have time for a quick look,' she said with a rather shaky smile she hoped was friendly. If they couldn't be lovers, then at least they could be friends and perhaps that would be enough.

'Come on in,' he said and turned back to his cottage.

She set Abby down and the little girl bounced ahead, leading the way and showing Laura with tremendous pride the patch of wall she'd been responsible for painting. 'Steve helped a teensy bit,' she announced, 'but I did most of it, didn't I, Steve?'

'You certainly did, princess,' he said, ruffling her hair affectionately.

Had he called his own child princess, or did he have some other pet name for her, Laura wondered. And why were there no photos on display?

'It looks great,' she said and it did, but she was hardly able to muster any enthusiasm. It could have been the most brilliantly decorated room in the world, but with all that was going on in her heart, she barely noticed.

'You were right about the colours.'

'Steve, I . . . I don't want you to think I'm not grateful for all you've done, but I spoke to Claire today and she's on the mend, so . . . ' Her voice trailed off. The last thing she wanted was to offend him, but to her surprise and delight, he was smiling.

'You won't be requiring my baby-sitting services any more,' he finished for her. 'Well, it was a pleasure while it lasted, but without my little helper, I should be able to get finished in half the time.

'You don't mind?' Laura breathed. Well that confounded all her theories about him wanting Abby to replace the child he'd lost. 'I thought . . . '

His eyes crinkled with laughter and a

tidal wave of relief washed over her.

'It's been great having her here, she's terrific company, don't get me wrong,' he said. 'Any time you need a baby-sitter, be sure to ask me first. Isn't that what friends are for?'

'Well . . . here, I knew you wouldn't accept payment of any kind, but I thought I should give you something,' she said, delving in her bag and producing a small parcel. 'It's just a little token. I don't know how I'd have managed without your help. I wasn't keen on sending Abby to someone I didn't know.'

His hands trembled as he took it and she was stabbed by the look of pleasure on his face. 'Aw, you shouldn't have,' he protested, but he still looked pleased as he unwrapped the parcel.

Her heart was hammering wildly. She hoped he liked it. It had been a spur of the moment buy and almost as soon as she got outside the shop, she began to have doubts. Was it the kind of gift a man like Steve would appreciate — any man come to that? His cottage had always struck her as being oddly devoid of those little things that make up a home and she'd thought, well she just thought it would look nice.

He opened the box and took out the china fox. 'It's beautiful,' he whispered. 'Really lovely.'

'Do you really like it?' she asked nervously.

'I love it,' he said, smiling readily. 'And it will remind me of these last couple of days with Abby. I'll put it here, on the mantelpiece.'

'We are friends then?' she asked uncertainly and he laughed.

'Friends,' he said. 'Good friends I hope, Laura.'

She was ridiculously pleased that he was pleased and could hardly wipe the smile off her face as she hurried home with Abby.

Abby was not so happy. 'It's not fair,' she said crossly. 'I don't want to go to Auntie Claire's, I want to stay with Steve.'

Laura was amazed at the outburst. Normally Abby was such a compliant child. This rebellious streak was something completely new and although it could create some difficulties, Laura welcomed it, for it signalled that Abby was finding new confidence in herself.

Steve waited until he heard Laura's front door close before he picked up the china fox. It really was beautiful. He'd neither wanted nor expected payment for taking care of Abby, but the gift had touched him more than he ever would have thought possible. But at least now he could get on with his decorating without interruptions. With a smile, he set the fox carefully down and prepared to start more painting.

8

Laura had hardly seen Steve since the day she collected Abby and gave him the china fox, but in that time, a change seemed to have come over him. He seemed less wary somehow and now it was time for their first antenatal session together, he was far more relaxed and friendly and she felt more at ease in his presence.

Maybe it was because of their agreement to be friends — just friends — it took the pressure off.

'Fancy a coffee upstairs before we start? If you're lucky I might even be able to find a chocolate chip cookie or two.' He rested his hand on her waist as they went towards the stairs. Laura felt her heart flutter and wished with all her being that he didn't have this effect on her, not when she'd made up her mind to settle for friendship.

Laura sat down in a chair by the window while Steve poured them both a coffee from the pot. It had turned out to be a dreary day, grey and windswept with icy rain lashing the windows. Even so, Laura felt a warm glow inside. She smiled up at Steve as he handed her a cup. 'Thanks.'

'It's your day off tomorrow, isn't it?' he asked, sitting down in the chair opposite hers and stretching out his long, lean legs. 'Mine, too. You hadn't anything special planned?'

'Just a quiet day. I thought I'd catch up on the ironing . . . '

She broke off, aware that he was watching her. His mouth looking warm and tempting. She hid her sudden dismay behind an angry expression.

'You look so funny when you're cross,' he teased.

Her heartbeat quickened and she set her cup down with a clatter. 'Don't play with me like this, Steve,' she said brokenly. 'It's not fair.'

'I'm not playing with you, love. I

wouldn't do that. I'd never do anything to hurt you, that's why — '

'Why you keep rejecting me?' Her heart was thundering as she waited for his answer. She hadn't meant to blurt that out and now she'd gone and spoiled everything again

'Is that what you think?' he whispered.

'Shouldn't we be getting downstairs?' she began. Coward, she thought. Running away just when you might be about to get some answers. But were they the answers she wanted to hear?

'No hurry,' he said. 'My first appointment isn't due for another ten minutes. This is far more important.'

'This isn't the time, Steve,' she said urgently. 'Or the place.'

'You're right.' He ran his hand through his hair and it flopped back into place. 'About this afternoon — we've got Tracey Marlow coming in.'

Laura welcomed the change of subject. 'She seems a nice, bright girl. Mature for her age, despite her predicament.'

There, she'd done it just as cleanly as he had, slipped into her professional shoes. She was astounded at how steady her voice came out, how calm she sounded when inside all hell was breaking loose.

They sat in companionable silence for a few moments, then Steve was speaking again. 'I was wondering, as we're both off tomorrow, would you and Abby like to . . . ?'

'I don't think so,' she said quickly before he could say any more. 'I won't be spending the day with Abby anyway. Claire and Mike are taking the children to stay with my parents for a few days, Abby included. Claire's still feeling a bit weak and she'll be spoiled rotten at Mum's.'

'So you'll be on your own then,' he mused.

Yes, on my own, Laura thought — so there, you're not interested now are you? Of course you're not. Laura Morgan just happens to be the mother of a child that reminds you too much of the child you lost. 'Shall we get down to the surgery?' she asked quickly, getting to her feet.

'Hold on. If Abby's away, then what's to stop the two of us going out together? I'd like to buy you dinner tomorrow night, and . . . ' he stopped and gazed at her so thoroughly that she absolutely tingled with embarrassment.

'I'm sorry, Steve,' she answered. 'but I can't go out with you.'

'Previous engagement?'

'No, I . . . ' She'd never been a very good liar and she wasn't making a very good job of it now.

'Are you afraid of me, Laura?' he asked gently and her heart went thud.

'Of course I'm not afraid of you,' she said. 'Your bark is far worse than your bite — and even that isn't that bad.'

'Then what? Is it Tim?'

She laughed incredulously. 'Tim?'

'You were in love with him once. Is there a part of you that still hopes he'll come back?'

'No,' she said firmly. 'Absolutely not.'

'Then come out with me. Let me buy you a meal, Laura. You'd love that new Greek restaurant in town, and I don't want to go alone.'

As if he had to when half the women in town would stampede for the chance to go with him. Laura couldn't remember the last time she'd been to a restaurant. Much as she adored her little cottage, it would be nice to get away for a change. And just one night wouldn't hurt.

'No strings, Laura. Just two good friends having a meal together.'

'All right,' she said. 'Put like that, how can I refuse?'

Had she really just agreed to go out with him? She must be crazy. Leaving him still standing by the window, she rushed out of the room and down the stairs into the relative safety of the reception area.

★   ★   ★

Laura sat at her dressing table, holding earrings up against her face, until she

138

found the right ones to compliment the black dress she wore. You're wasting your time, she kept telling herself over and over. But there was nothing on earth could stop the thread of joy winding its way through her body, leaving her glowing and happy as she hurried down the stairs.

In the soft glow of the hall light, Steve's hair shone and Laura's breath caught. He looked so handsome and debonair in an inky black suit and gleaming white shirt. His smile was no less devastating than his appearance and when it reached his eyes, they twinkled like stars.

'You look gorgeous,' he breathed at last.

'I'll just get my coat,' she said. 'Come in.'

She turned her back to him and rushed to fetch her coat from the hall closet, feeling his eyes boring into her every step of the way. She returned carrying her coat over her arm. He took it from her and without a word, held it up. As she slid her hands into the sleeves, he took a step nearer and gently brushed the nape of her neck with his lips. She trembled and the brief, gentle touch of his lips was remembered long after he'd slipped the coat onto her shoulders. As they moved towards the door, he reached out to switch off the lights and at the same time managed somehow to enfold her in his arms.

'You're so lovely,' he murmured huskily.

'Don't,' she pleaded. She couldn't bear to have him raising her spirits, firing her desire only to shoot her down in flames when things got too hot for him to handle. 'Just friends, remember,' she reminded him.

'If that's what you want,' he said, but his eyes were saying something totally different.

Her heart was thudding painfully. She could feel his warm breath against her cheek and longed for his kiss, despite all the frantic warnings her churning mind was issuing.

'Oh, Laura . . .' he whispered urgently, his mouth grazing her cheek before finding her mouth and claiming it.

Laura felt dizzy as a multitude of sensations crashed through her body. All her senses were aflame, but her will was limp. Whatever he asked of her, she would willingly give. She was his, no matter what, his to claim whenever and wherever he wanted.

At last he pulled away. 'We have to go. Better hold on to me,' he said as they left the cottage. 'It's pretty slippery underfoot.'

The ground was still wet from an earlier storm and leaves everywhere made the ground slippery as ice. She slipped her arm through his and held on as they walked over to his car. He opened the passenger door, settled her in her seat, then closed it and hurried round to his own side.

'Warm enough?' he said, glancing at her. 'I can turn the heat up a bit if you feel cold.' But she was already warm right through from the marrow in her bones to her flushed, soft skin. 'I expect Abby was looking forward to staying with her grandparents,' he said. 'She talked about them quite a lot while she was with me.'

'Dad spoils her,' she said, smiling. 'And Abby does like to be spoiled.'

'What about her own father?'

'Tim?' She laughed bitterly.

'Laura, don't you think it's wrong to stop him seeing her? She told me he'd gone away and she never sees him, but surely . . . ?'

'You think I'd deliberately stand between them?' Laura cried. 'I'd have given anything to have him show some kind of interest in Abby. I told you he didn't want her. There was no miracle change in him after she was born.' It hurt her to think that he could think she'd stoop so low as to keep a child from seeing her father, or vice versa. 'And how dare you question Abby about her father?'

'I didn't. She volunteered the information. When my wife was leaving me,

142

she left a note telling me not to try tracing her. She suggested I forget I ever had a wife and daughter.'

Laura gasped. This was the first time he'd ever spoken of Tricia and Lucy to her and she held her breath, waiting for him to continue, wondering if she should say anything or just listen.

'She made damn sure I never saw Lucy again,' he said.

'I know,' Laura said softly and she reached out to gently touch his arm and was surprised when he shuddered. 'I'm so sorry, Steve.'

'You know?'

'About Tricia and Lucy . . . and the river. I've only just found out, otherwise . . . well, I said a few things which must have been hurtful. I'm sorry.'

'Lucy didn't want to go,' he said. 'She ran away — down to the river. She thought she might find me on the boat, but she slipped . . . ' He braked harshly, then he just sat totally still, staring ahead, breathing hard. He gave a short, bitter laugh. 'Why do I feel so guilty?

For the first time in — God knows — years I suppose, I've felt whole again. I've felt that maybe life was worth living after all . . . '

'What's wrong with that?' Her voice was gentle and filled with concern.

'I had everything a man could want once, Laura — and I lost it all.'

'That wasn't your fault,' she said vehemently. 'No more than it was mine or Tim's fault that our marriage failed.'

'Maybe not, but if I'd handled things better. If I'd given her the freedom she craved maybe my little girl would still be alive today.'

'Oh, love.' So many times she'd longed to hold him and this time she had to give in to her feelings. She leaned across the car and put her arms around his rigid body, resting her head against his shoulder. If only he'd give her the chance, she'd never ask for her freedom, for to be bound to him for eternity would be heaven as far as she was concerned. Lifting her head slightly, she realised he was looking down at her and as she tilted her face to his, their lips met in the most tender of kisses.

It wasn't his grief she was fighting here — but his guilt. The realisation of that hit her like a hammer blow. The tension flooded out of him as he stopped fighting and returned her kiss, his mouth closing over hers. It brought her to her senses. She'd meant to comfort him, not end up in a passionate clinch. She drew back.

'What is it?'

'It's Abby,' she said. 'Is she . . . does she remind you of Lucy?'

There was a dreadful heavy silence. She couldn't see his face in the darkness, but she could sense the sudden tension. Surely to God, she hadn't put her foot in it yet again?

'Abby's nothing like Lucy. Nothing at all,' he said. 'Surely you don't think . . . ? You do, don't you? You think I'm only interested in Abby because she reminds me of Lucy? You're wrong, so wrong.' He twisted the key in the

145

ignition. 'We'd better get on. I've got a table booked.'

Every time she thought she was getting close to him, he threw up a huge impenetrable wall between them, but she was just as bad and it was back there again, twice as thick as ever and impossible to break down.

* * *

Steve pulled up in the car park outside Andreas' Greek Taverna and turned to face her. Even in the shadows, she could see he was smiling. 'Have you ever been to Greece, Laura?'

'I'm afraid not.'

'Then prepare yourself,' he laughed softly.

They were immediately drawn into the warmth of the restaurant and Laura had the immediate impression of a lively, happy atmosphere. Greek music played as a background to the murmur of contented chatter and the clinking of glasses. She slipped her hand nervously into Steve's and he squeezed it reassuringly.

'Dr Drake, and your lovely companion.'

'Laura, allow me to introduce Andreas,' Steve said with a grin, as Andreas stooped to kiss the back of her hand.

'Please, this way.'

Andreas led them to a table, waited until they were seated, and then handed them each a menu.

'I will be back shortly,' Andreas announced proudly and bustled away.

'This is wonderful,' she said.

'The food is excellent and Andreas has a knack of making everyone who walks through the door feel special. Now, what shall we start with?'

Laura considered the menu. 'Taramasalata with crispy toast and olives,' she said without hesitation.

'I like a girl who knows her own mind,' he remarked.

'Oh, I have no trouble knowing my own mind,' she replied. 'It's other people's I have a problem with.'

'Mine?' His eyebrows rose and he gave her a quirky smile. Steve ordered the meal, and a bottle of wine, which Laura seemed to drink all on her own.

Steve thought of Tricia, of her constant diets, her finicky eating habits. She was obsessed with her weight, her looks, everything about herself. It was a blessing that Lucy had been born beautiful, for everything had to be perfect in order that Tricia should love it.

'Tonight it was a sheer delight to eat.' Laura said, not noticing the sudden darkening of his expression. 'I can't remember the last time I enjoyed a meal so much.'

He shook his head, forced his mind to the present. 'Neither can I,' he said. 'Nor enjoyed a woman's company so much.'

Laura thrilled at his words. Soothed by the wine, she allowed herself to believe he could actually mean them. They were, both of them, casualties of love, but they were different people now. More mature, moulded by life. The past was irrelevant, light years away.

'Laura, there's something I must . . .'

Andreas was on his way back and the moment was lost.

'I have to talk to you,' Steve whispered urgently and something about his tone, his expression chilled her. 'I want to set your mind at rest as far as Lucy and Abby are concerned. But not here.'

The feeling of dread didn't last long. Laura was warmed through with the wine and bad or sad thoughts were not allowed to enter her mind.

* * *

When he pulled up outside their cottages, Steve said, 'You will come in for a coffee before you go home?' It was more a command than a request.

She slipped and almost fell on the path outside his house, but his arm was around her in an instant, holding her steady until he'd thrust his key into the

149

lock and they were inside. The house smelled of fresh paint.

'Make yourself comfortable,' he said, opening the door to the sitting room. 'I'll get the coffee.'

While he was gone, Laura threw herself into an armchair.

He looked troubled when he came in with the coffee.

She would never have thought it possible for someone like Steve to look so vulnerable, so terribly lost. And then he left suddenly and went upstairs. Laura heard his feet crossing the bedroom above her head. Was she supposed to follow him? Perplexed, she stayed right where she was awaiting his return. When he came back he was carrying a framed photograph. Wordlessly, he handed it to her.

Laura gasped. 'This was Tricia and Lucy?' she whispered. 'They're beautiful. Your daughter was a truly lovely little girl.'

He flinched. 'Lucy wasn't my daughter. I've never told anyone else. It didn't stop me being devastated when she died.'

'When . . . when did you find out?'

'The day I lost her. It was all in Tricia's farewell note — the truth. In the days that followed, I prayed that Lucy would, by some miracle, be found alive. I vowed that she'd never find out the truth, that I wasn't her father, but I was never given the chance. We were on the point of splitting up when Tricia told me she was pregnant. I've always taken marriage seriously, Laura and at first, things seemed to be working out. Tricia tried, I tried and for a while we were happy.'

'Why are you telling me all this?' she asked.

'Because I want you to stop comparing me with Tim. You may not think you are, but he's there, like a phantom from your past, haunting you. Don't you think he's hurt you enough? Let him go, Laura.'

'And then what?' she asked, her voice trembling.

'Then make a fresh start, you and Abby.'

'And you? Where do you fit in to all this, Steve?'

'I'm not sure that I do. The way I feel about you it wouldn't be long before we were making some kind of commitment.'

'I thought you were only interested in me because of Abby,' she said again, almost to herself. It wouldn't be fair to tell him that Caroline had put that idea in her head. She said, 'You seem so fond of her, so afraid for her.'

'I am fond of her,' he replied. 'She's a terrific kid — in her own right, Laura, not because she reminds me of Lucy, or makes me realise what I've lost. No, it's something quite different to that. I think, through Abby, I've realised that life does go on. And yes, when it comes to the river, I am afraid. At first I just didn't want to see another tragedy, then as I came to know the two of you better . . . Hell, Laura, I just didn't want to see another human being have to go through what I went through — I didn't want to see you get hurt.'

'Would it make any difference to the way you feel if I told you I loved you?' she said softly. No sooner were the words out than she could have kicked herself. What was she doing, laying herself bare like this, opening herself up to all kinds of hurt and pain?

He looked astonished. 'Are we speaking figuratively?' he asked, giving her the chance to save herself from digging a hole too deep to climb out of.

'Of course,' she said quickly, then was angry for not having the courage to stick to her guns. If he were to find out how she really felt about him, it would make a complete mockery of all her protestations to the contrary.

'Good,' he said. 'I'm glad, Laura.'

But what happened next made liars of both of them.

She moved towards him, drawn by some invisible force, and he welcomed her into his embrace, his kisses like fire against her skin until his mouth claimed hers and she was lost to her reeling senses. A voice inside her head told her she was a fool, but Laura ignored it. She told herself as she surrendered to his kisses that she was just a woman with a woman's needs and there was nothing wrong in answering those needs. The voice told her that she'd hate herself in the morning, but a louder voice said she didn't care. A sob rose in her throat, but it wasn't an unhappy sound. Far from it.

9

When she woke the next morning amid a tangle of sheets, it was to find herself alone in the bed. She climbed out of bed dragging a sheet with her and shivered as the dawn chill touched her shoulders with icy fingers. From the bedroom window she could see the river like a silver snake moving slowly beyond the trees.

'Steve,' she called softly and a thread of fear trickled slowly down her spine. Where was he? Perhaps he'd been called out to an emergency, but she hadn't heard the phone ring. Fear growing inside her, mushrooming into something horrible and big and overwhelming, she went carefully down the stairs, the sheet bundled around her body.

Steve was in the sitting room with his back to her. As she approached she realised he had something in his hand.

It was the photograph of Tricia and Lucy, the one he'd brought downstairs to show her last night.

Startled by her sudden intake of breath, he turned sharply and she saw the dampness of tears under his eyes. He'd lied. He did love Tricia. He was just trying to kid himself and her that he didn't and he'd used her in an attempt to exorcise the ghosts that haunted him.

'Laura . . .' He started to his feet, the picture dropped to the floor and the glass in the frame shattered.

'No.' she cried. 'Don't touch me, don't come near me.' And with that, she fled up the stairs sobbing her heart out, determined now that he should never get close to her again.

He was too stunned to follow, instead stooping to gather up the shards of glass that littered the carpet. He knew she'd regret it. He'd known all along, yet last night he'd allowed passion to get the better of him. His attempts to explain to Laura his reasons for not wanting to get involved obviously hadn't sunk in. She'd drunk too much with the meal, that was all, but he'd been sober, stone cold sober and should have had more control.

By the time he went upstairs, she was dressed and shoving her feet furiously into her shoes. 'Laura, I'm sorry . . . '

'Don't you dare apologise,' she snapped. 'I just don't know where I am with you from one minute to the next!'

'I shouldn't have taken advantage,' he said raggedly.

'For God's sake!' She cried. 'I wish you'd get it through your head that — oh, never mind! You never listen to anything I say anyway. I'm going away, Steve. I'm going to join Abby at my parents' house. I'll call Caroline and get her to arrange emergency cover for me at the Lodge.'

'You don't have to go,' he said quietly.

'Don't be ridiculous,' she said and brushed past him. 'Just do something for me.'

'Anything.'

'Keep an eye on Sam. Feed him.' Somehow she managed to gather up the few remaining shreds of her pride and hurry out.

Steve stood at the bedroom window watching as she hauled a bag out of her cottage and tossed it into the boot of her car.

He'd done it again in grand style. He'd blown it. Fate had thrown him a lifeline, a last chance at happiness and he'd tossed it right back again. All he ever wanted to do was to avoid hurting her and that's precisely what he'd achieved and in the worst possible way.

★ ★ ★

Laura returned to work just over a week later. She'd done a lot of thinking while she was away and knew there was only one thing she could do. She opened the paper and, as fate would have it, it fell open at the appointments section. With a red pen and an aching heart, she began to circle jobs that appealed, the main criteria being that they were as far away from Banford Mills — and Steve Drake — as possible.

* * *

The early morning post brought two application forms. Laura was on her way to work and took them with her, intending to fill them in during her break and get them sent off as quickly as possible.

She hadn't mentioned the possibility of a move to Claire or to Abby for, as far as her daughter was concerned, she was anxious that another upheaval in her young life might have far-reaching consequences. Should Abby really have to pay for Laura's mistakes? It didn't seem very fair, but what other choice did she have? How could she go on working with Steve when every time she saw him, she felt as if her heart was being ripped out?

Laura opened out one of the application forms and filled in her name. The position was at a hospital in the Midlands where she'd be just one more midwife on a large team. She didn't want to leave Banford Mills, her home or her job. But it was a case of self preservation.

When the door opened and Steve walked in, she blushed deeply, glad her thoughts about him had been silent.

'Welcome back,' his tone was just off being brusque and he had a wary look in his eyes.

'Thank you, Doctor.'

'What happened to Steve?' he said, making her heart ache even more.

'Things are different now,' she said. 'I'd hate you to think I was throwing myself at you again, so I think it would be better all round if we keep our relationship strictly professional.'

'If that's how you want it,' he remarked so huskily she barely heard.

No, that's not how I want it, a voice inside her head screamed, that's just the way it has to be.

'While I'm here,' he went on. 'Could

I see Miss Dowe's notes?'

'I'll just get them,' Laura said, rising to her feet. The files were all kept in a locked cabinet in the corridor behind a desk that was rarely used. Laura hurried out of the office, trying to ignore the fact that Steve was watching her every movement. When she returned, he'd turned the application form she'd left on her desk around and was reading what she'd written so far. She placed the file down on top of it, but it was too late to hope he hadn't seen.

Frowning, he took hold of her hand and she hadn't the will to pull away. 'I . . . I felt it was time to move on,' she blustered.

'To this?' He moved the file and lifted the application form. 'To a large hospital where half the time you won't know the names of your patients? That's not you, Laura. You took the post here to get away from that.'

His voice was rough. Coming to her senses, she jerked her hand away and snatched the application form back.

'How do you know what's right for me and what isn't?' she demanded.

'I know you,' he said, his frown deepening. 'Perhaps better than you think. You're not keen to move on. You were happy here until I ruined everything. Isn't that right?'

He'd hit the nail squarely on the head. Her heart was bumping so loud and hard against her ribs, it was a wonder he couldn't hear it. Reaching out, he took the application form, tore it in two, then dropped it in the bin.

'What did you do that for?' she asked, wide-eyed at his presumption.

'I'm stopping you from making the biggest mistake of your life,' he said.

'Thanks for the advice,' she replied, amazing herself with how calm and cool she sounded. 'But I think I'm capable of making up my own mind about what's best for me.'

She didn't quite understand herself why she hadn't absolutely boiled over with rage when he tore her application up. A simple phone call would bring

through to Abby's room. She looked like a little cherub in the soft glow of the night lamp. Laura had tried to get her to sleep without it, but it was a childish insecurity that Abby clung to and while she needed it, Laura was quite happy to leave it.

★   ★   ★

In the morning as she was leaving for work, Steve came strolling along the path out of the mist towards her. This was Steve as she'd never seen him before; sombre, dressed entirely in black and wearing a leather jacket.

'Steve.' Abby squealed delightedly and flung herself into his arms.

His serious face broke into a smile and, lifting her high in the air he swung her round and then kissed the tip of her nose. 'How're you doing, princess?' he asked. 'Did you have a good holiday?'

She wrinkled her nose, cast a look that held an apology at her mother and blurted, 'I did, but Mummy didn't.'

Laura knew what was coming next, but was powerless to stop the words tumbling from Abby's mouth. 'Mummy cried every night we were away.'

She tried, oh, God how she'd tried to hide the tears from her daughter, but it had been difficult as they had to share a bed. She thought she'd succeeded, but obviously she hadn't.

'It was 'cause she missed Sam,' Abby explained.

Reluctantly she dragged her eyes up to meet his and the look she saw there made her knees buckle. 'Come on, Abby, we have to go,' Laura said and Steve put the little girl down and she scampered towards the car.

She'd never seen him looking as sexy as he did this morning. Black suited him. It made his tousled fair hair seem brighter and the dark shadow of stubble on his face gave him a dangerously attractive look. Oh, no you don't, Laura told herself as she reined in her thoughts which seemed determined to go their own sweet way.

'Laura,' he called her back as she started off behind Abby. 'You haven't applied for any more jobs, have you?'

She lowered her eyes and laughed softly. 'No. You were right, it wouldn't be fair to uproot Abby when she's just getting settled.'

'I'm glad,' he said softly.

Remaining where he was, he looked down at her, but she couldn't meet his gaze. What right did he have to hurt her like this? It simply wasn't fair. 'Are you?' She looked up, her smoky eyes smouldering with doubt and fear and some feeling she didn't even recognise.

'Drive carefully. There have been warnings about the fog on the radio.'

'I always drive carefully,' she replied.

He nodded, but made no reply, so she hurried away leaving him standing there looking gorgeous and wonderful and so damned unattainable.

10

Arriving at the Lodge, Laura found an ambulance outside, its doors wide open. She broke into a run, heart hammering as she burst into the Lodge to find Caroline rushing along beside a trolley being pushed by a green jacketed paramedic.

'Laura — hurry.' Caroline called. 'This is Tracey Marlow, she's — '

'Tracey!' Laura cried. She stopped beside the trolley and turned to the paramedic. 'You've brought her to the wrong hospital,' she said urgently.

'We couldn't get her to the General. The roads are blocked. There's been a bad pile up.'

'What about other routes?'

'What other routes?' he said ruefully. 'The Banford Mills road has been closed for over a week. The only other route is across the river, but the bridge is under repair.'

'Sister Morgan,' Tracey cried and flung out her hand to grasp Laura's. Her relief upon seeing a friendly, familiar face heartbreakingly obvious. 'It hurts, Sister, it hurts.'

'All right, sweetheart,' Laura said. 'You'll be fine now.'

'I want my dad,' she cried in a tiny voice. 'Where's my dad?'

'He's on his way, love,' the paramedic said. 'What do you want us to do, Sister? Hang on here and hope they clear the roads, or what?'

Laura thought quickly. 'Go back to the ambulance station,' she said at last. 'If the worst comes to the worst, we can get a helicopter.'

'In this weather?' he returned doubtfully.

'It can't stay foggy all day,' Laura said hopefully. 'Caroline, call Dr Drake immediately. Make sure you tell him that it's an emergency.'

'I'm frightened,' Tracey whispered as Laura pushed her into the delivery suite. 'It's too early. The baby's coming too early.'

The paramedic helped Laura move Tracey onto the bed, then wheeled the trolley away.

'Relax, sweetheart. I want you to breathe deeply, in through your nose . . . two . . . three and out, gently, slowly.' Spending a little time now giving her a quick lesson in breathing, could pay dividends later on. When Tracey had the rhythm of the deep breathing, Laura told her she may have to pant during the labour and explained why.

By the time Caroline joined her, Laura was examining Tracey. 'Try not to worry too much about it being early,' Laura said. 'We've an incubator here.'

Caroline whispered, 'Her father is outside. What do we do with him?'

'Is it my dad?' Tracey half sat up. 'Did you say he was here? Can he come in, please, Sister. I want my dad.'

'I'll get him,' Laura said without hesitation.

The burly man pacing the corridor outside looked up, his weather beaten features, ragged with worry. 'How is she?' He stepped forward and in a completely unconscious gesture, he grasped Laura's hands in his, crushing her small bones, making her wince with pain.

'The baby is very early, Mr Marlow,' Laura explained gently. 'It will be tiny and will need specialist care. At the moment, Tracey is coping very well. I've given her something to relieve the pain.'

He was hanging on her every word. 'She will be all right though, won't she? I mean, even if the baby doesn't make it . . .'

'I hope they'll both make it, Mr Marlow,' Laura smiled. 'Now she'd like you with her. Do you think you can cope? It could be very upsetting for you to see your daughter in so much pain, but I think if you could be there with her, it would help.'

'Of course,' he said. 'Do I have to wear one of those funny hats?'

'Oh, yes,' Laura laughed. 'I'm afraid you do. And a gown. What Tracey needs is encouragement. There may be moments when you feel like screaming, but if you stay calm and relaxed, it really will help.'

'All right, Sister,' he nodded eagerly. 'Anything you say. I just want my little girl to be all right. She's my world.'

'I'll get Caroline to get you ready, then she'll bring you in.'

Laura couldn't help thinking how confident and capable she sounded, when deep inside she was quite concerned. He released her hands and gave her a sheepish smile, then she turned away, flexing her fingers as she went, knowing she'd have a few bruises tomorrow.

She could have wept with relief when Steve walked in. He wasn't hurrying, but came in with his usual loping stride, but Laura knew he must have rushed to get here so quickly. This calm, laid back approach was entirely for Mr Marlow's benefit.

'Hello, Mr Marlow,' he said, acknowledging Laura with a brief nod as he spoke. 'Don't worry about Tracey. She's in the very best of hands with Sister Morgan.'

As Caroline arrived and led Mr Marlow away, Laura rounded on Steve. 'It's so early,' she said desperately. 'And she's so young.'

'I have every faith in you, Laura. We can do this.' With that, he turned and went into the delivery suite and at once his voice took on that light, cheerful tone she knew so well. 'Hello, Tracey. What happened? Couldn't you wait to have your baby?'

Laura arranged her features into an expression of calm capability and followed him.

Tracey was a surprisingly strong and resilient young woman, and Laura marvelled at her composure under these extreme circumstances. Even more wonderful, was the relationship between father and daughter. Mr Marlow obviously doted on his only child and while Laura knew he must be going through agonies himself, he remained cheerful and encouraging all the way through.

At last the tiny head was crowned, the frail little body following quickly behind. Laura couldn't put the baby onto his mother's stomach as she would normally, but took him immediately to the examination table. As Steve examined him, the baby let out a weak cry which had everyone in the room laughing with relief.

Laura looked up and her eyes met Steve's. For a moment, it was as if they were of one mind, sharing a spirit, laughing together in this special, wonderful moment. The baby was not out of danger and for at least a few days, if not weeks, he was going to have to struggle for his very survival, but he was already a little fighter.

'He needs specialist treatment,' Steve said. 'Now the fog's clearing a bit, I'm going to see if I can get the helicopter down here.'

Despite the cold and damp, people came out of the hospital to watch as they were whisked away by the helicopter that had landed briefly in the hospital grounds. There wasn't a window that didn't have at least four faces pressed to it and, as the helicopter rose into the sky, there wasn't a person watching who wasn't praying for the young mother and her baby.

'I'm better be going home,' Mr Marlow said gruffly. 'There's nothing else for me to do here.'

'She'll be all right, Mr Marlow,' Laura said. 'She's a strong girl.'

'She's my girl,' he said, his voice trembling with pride. 'And for what he's put her through, I could kill that lad.'

Seeing Laura's sudden look of concern, he chuckled softly and added, 'Don't worry, I won't lay a finger on him. She'd never forgive me if I did. I'm going there now to tell him he's got a son — and God help him if he ever lets them down.'

Laura watched him go. Steve had gone in the helicopter with Tracey and the baby. They'd be arriving at the specialist baby unit within minutes and little baby Marlow would benefit from the best treatment. She drew in a deep shuddering breath and hurried back into the Lodge.

Before she left for home, there was good news from the General. Little Stephen Marlow was holding his own. Laura practically floated all the way to Claire's to collect Abby, she was so happy.

'You look a bit more cheerful than you did this morning,' Claire commented. 'Are things any easier between you and Steve?'

While they had been away, Laura had given her older sister an abbreviated version of the situation with her and Steve.

'Not easier,' Laura sighed. 'Different perhaps. I don't know.'

'If you love him and he loves you, then you'll get together eventually.'

'That's the problem,' Laura had said unhappily. 'He doesn't love me. He's still in love with his wife.'

'I don't think so,' Claire disagreed.

Now she was looking at her little sister with motherly concern and Laura smiled quickly. 'I've accepted that where Steve and I are concerned, there'll be no happy ever after.'

★ ★ ★

Later, when Abby was sound asleep in bed, Laura curled up in an armchair and closed her eyes only to be startled by a tapping at the door.

'Sam,' she muttered. 'Why can't you use the flap like any normal cat?'

She'd never known such a daft cat. Mike had put a cat flap in the back door on the day they moved in, but in their last home, Sam had always come in and out by the door or window and he saw no reason to change the habits of a lifetime.

Sam rushed in as soon as the door

was opened and Laura said, 'I wish you'd use the cat flap.'

'I think I'm a bit large to fit through that small opening,' Steve chuckled softly and her heart did a double somersault.

'What are you doing here?' she cried.

'I came to see you,' he said. 'I thought you'd like to hear the latest about Tracey and the baby. I've just got back.'

'Come in,' she said, practically dragging him through the door she was so eager for news.

He half fell into the chair by the fire. 'I'm frozen,' he said, rubbing his hands together. He was so cold, his teeth were chattering.

'How did it go?'

'The baby — she's naming him Stephen, by the way,' he said with a roguish grin which Laura couldn't help but return. 'He's in the special baby care unit and they're very pleased with him so far.'

'I called the hospital earlier,' she

admitted. 'They said they were very hopeful. How long will she have to stay there?'

'They're going to keep Tracey there for at least ten days. Poor kid. Wasn't she great?' His voice shook with pride.

She took his frozen hands in hers and gently rubbed warmth into them.

'If you had any sense at all, you'd stop that right now,' he growled softly. 'Otherwise I won't be answerable to the consequences.'

'What consequences?'

He pulled his hands away and gently ran his fingers through her hair, holding her head steady so he could kiss her.

He could hurt her all he wanted, she just didn't care any more; the way she loved him made it impossible for her to have any will of her own.

Abby's voice from upstairs had them springing apart guiltily.

'I'll go,' he said, stumbling to his feet. He looked shell-shocked, confused. With her own thoughts in a state of disarray, Laura had every sympathy with him. What were they to do? Was there no way out of this mess for them?

He seemed to be gone an age and when she eventually followed him upstairs, it was to find him sitting on the edge of Abby's bed. He was singing to her, his voice soft and deep and Laura stood out on the landing, gripping the rail at the top of the stairs for support.

'Sweet dreams, princess,' he said softly as he stooped and kissed Abby's forehead. He came out of the room and closed the door behind him.

'She's asleep,' he whispered. 'Out like a light. Apparently Sam jumped on her bed and woke her up.'

'Darn cat,' Laura muttered.

'Maybe he did us a favour,' he murmured, his fingers absently toying with the coils of her dark hair as he spoke. 'We're not safe to be left alone together, are we, Laura?'

'It seems not,' she agreed shakily.

'I just find it absolutely incredible that you still want anything to do with me after the way I've treated you.'

'That's easily explained,' she sighed. 'I love you.'

His fingers stiffened and his face crumpled. 'Oh, Laura, my love. After all I've put you through, you can say that . . .'

'I mean it,' she declared, then went on in a mad rush, 'I know you don't want a relationship right now, least of all with a woman who has a child, but . . .' And that's just about when her resolve gave way and all the pain and grief of the past few days proved too much and she burst into tears.

He didn't put his arms around her this time, but gently tilted her chin so she had to look at him, and what she saw reflected in his eyes was all the love she had so longed to see. But was it real or imagined? Was she so crazy about him that she could no longer tell the difference?

There never was a bigger fool to walk the earth than him he thought as he trailed his finger gently across her soft, flushed cheek. He searched her eyes, as if he could probe the misty grey depths and see what was etched into her soul.

Abby murmured in her sleep and it prompted them both to move at once, hurrying down the stairs and returning to the sitting room.

'That night we spent together . . . ' he began, but had to break off, for the memory of that night was more than he could bear. 'I thought that was it, that it would be happy ever after for us, that you loved me as much as I loved you. I've never felt so happy in all my life, but then you came downstairs and you seemed so mad, so angry . . . It was as if you hated me.'

'But you were looking at Tricia's picture and . . . you were crying,' she said. 'I thought you were regretting . . . '

'I don't regret a single moment with you,' he said fiercely. 'I was looking at that picture trying to conjure up some kind of feeling . . . I don't know

. . . guilt, remorse, regret, but there was nothing there, nothing at all. They weren't tears of sorrow, Laura, they were tears of relief and joy because I realised I was free to love again and was no longer shackled to the past.'

'Then why did you let me go? Why didn't you tell me?'

'Because I thought you were mad at me for taking advantage of you.' His words were like hammer blows to her heart, exquisitely painful.

'You didn't, can't you see? I knew exactly what I was doing . . .' She touched his face, igniting a flame within him that seemed to consume his entire being and he shook from head to toe.

Reaching out, he gently took her hands in his and pulled her into his arms. 'Oh, my love,' he murmured, his lips caressing her hair as he spoke. 'If you only knew how much you mean to me, how much I love you . . .'

'Tell me,' she whispered hoarsely.

'I love you, Laura,' he said. 'Will you marry me?'

'Yes,' she whispered, wanting more than anything else to be with him, knowing that this time it was real, this time it would be forever.